PRAISE FOR THE W

M000073735

"Alan Baxter's fiction is dark, disturbing, hard-hitting and heart-breakingly honest. He reflects on worlds known and unknown with compassion, and demonstrates an almost second-sight into human behaviour."

— **Kaaron Warren, Shirley Jackson Award-winner and author of *The Grief Hole***

"Alan Baxter is an accomplished storyteller who ably evokes magic and menace."

— **Laird Barron, author of *Swift to Chase***

"Alan's work is reminiscent of that of Clive Barker and Jim C. Hines, but with a unique flavour all of its own."

— **Angela Slatter, World Fantasy, British Fantasy and Aurealis Award winner**

"Alan Baxter has joined the ranks of talented authors who seek to push the boundaries of fantasy fiction."

— *The Manly Daily*

"Alan Baxter delivers a heady mix of magic, monsters and bloody fights to the death. Nobody does kick-ass brutality like Baxter."

— **Greig Beck, International bestselling author of *Beneath the Dark Ice* and *Primordia***

"If Stephen King and Jim Butcher ever had a love child then it would be Alan Baxter."

— *Smash Dragons*

"Baxter draws you along a knife's edge of tension from the first page to the last, leaving your heart thumping and sweat on your brow."

— *Midwest Book Review*

MANIFEST RECALL

ALAN BAXTER

This novel remains
the copyright of the author.

MANIFEST RECALL
ISBN-13: 978-1-940658-95-7
ISBN-10: 1-940658-95-0
Grey Matter Press First Trade Paperback Edition - June 2018

Copyright © 2018 Alan Baxter
Cover Artwork Copyright © 2018 Sabercore Art
Book Design Copyright © 2018 Grey Matter Press
Edited by Anthony Rivera

GREY MATTER
P R E S S

CHICAGO

Grey Matter Press
greymatterpress.com

Grey Matter Press on Facebook
facebook.com/greymatterpress

MANIFEST RECALL

ALAN BAXTER

"THE SOULS THAT THRONG THE FLOOD
ARE THOSE TO WHOM, BY FATE, ARE OTHER BODIES OW'D:
IN LETHE'S LAKE THEY LONG OBLIVION TASTE,
OF FUTURE LIFE SECURE, FORGETFUL OF THE PAST."

The Aeneid (Book VI), **Virgil, 19 BCE**

ONE

I BOUGHT A USED CAR OFF A WOMAN as thin as her hand-rolled cigarettes. "It's a good price," I told her. "Why are you selling?"

"Last year," she said, beginning to tremble, "I had a business and a husband. Now I have neither. I can't wake up in the middle of the night any more, unable to breathe, panicking about debt."

I remember that clearly. Her wide, bloodshot eyes, her stained teeth and rat-tail hair. I feel it like a weight on me, my sympathy for that terrible, mundane predicament. It's indelible that memory. So I know exactly who I got this car from, even if I have no idea where it happened. Or when. Or where I am now.

Or who the hell this shivering girl beside me might be.

Her knees are pulled up to her chest, dirty bare feet on the seat, arms wrapped around her shins. She's wearing her seat belt, and her hands are secured together at the wrists with a black plastic cable tie. All that I see from the corner of my eye.

I dare not turn to look directly at her. Not yet. She stares ahead through the windshield, unmoving. Her face is almost as dirty as her feet and she's wearing an oversized T-shirt. Whether she has on shorts or only underwear underneath, or even nothing at all, I can't tell.

The road ahead is dark, no streetlights, only the car's headlights spiking onto the grey, dirty asphalt. Trees flicker by on either side, occasionally a glimpse of stars in the night sky when the canopy over the road briefly breaks.

Where the hell am I?

I feel as though I've just been switched on, like a light in an old house, flooding a room with illumination for the first time in years. Or ever. A flicker of story from Greek mythology comes to me. Lethe. One of five rivers in the underworld of Hades, the river of unmindfulness. The shades of the dead were required to drink its waters in order to forget their earthly life. Maybe I've died and drunk a gutful of Lethe and this is some strange Hell.

I need to take it back a bit. Instead of trying to figure out why I can't remember all this stuff, let's see what I *can* remember. Can I remember anything?

My name is Eli Carver.

I'm twenty-eight years old.

I killed a man in New Orleans and it made me vomit.

Jesus fuck, I put that gun against his ear and pulled the trigger and his head exploded like a fucking watermelon. I can still see my hand trembling as I did it, recall the wash of terror and disgust. I didn't want to do it, but something made me. Some*one* made me. It was a hot night, a warm breeze blowing gently across that balcony overlooking Bourbon Street, carrying the aromas of fried food and cigar smoke. My knees were knocking like saplings in a gale. But I did it. I killed him.

"You back, you fucking weirdo?"

Her voice startles me out of my thoughts and the car weaves slightly left and right.

"Don't drive off the fucking road and kill us now, you dick."

She's still staring straight ahead, still clutching her knees. Her voice is hard, hateful.

I glance across at her, she can't be more than eighteen or nineteen. "Back?"

"You've been a robot since Vernon's, man. You gotta pull it together."

She clearly knows more than I do, but I can hardly ask her to fill me in. Can I? She's the one tied up and filthy. I'm driving. Have I kidnapped her? I suck a long breath in through my nose and try to stay calm, act like I'm not a blank page in an empty notebook. Vernon's, she said. Do I know any Vernons?

"Can you at least turn the damn heater on?"

It is cold in the car and I'm wearing jeans and boots and a short denim jacket over a black T-shirt. No wonder she's shivering. I crank up the heat and it blasts from the vents in an instant, warm and musty, stinking of burned oil. Maybe this car isn't what it used to be. In the memory of buying it, the thing was almost new, smelled of air freshener and the seats were clean. That must have been a long time ago and I obviously had some money back then. I'm not sure what's in my pocket now.

And it's cold, but the night I shot that guy was warm. How much time has passed? He was the first, I realize, long ago. But not the last. He was the catalyst, the one who changed me. Here and now, this night, this dark road, was kick-started *that* night as I turned and vomited into a potted palm on that sweaty balcony. Someone laughing, saying, "Damn, kid, I didn't think you had it in you. Thought we'd be burying two bodies tonight."

And through the haze of my vomit tears I see the broad back of a man with a bald head, trailing acrid cigar smoke, walking back through double leadlight doors into the house. His shoulders move as he's still laughing to himself. Vernon. Vernon Sykes, mobster extraordinaire. Of course. That's him, but I can't see his face. Still can't remember that. Two burly guys clap me on the back, one says, "That puking will stop. You'll get used to it."

It's not something I ever want to get used to.

"We got this," the other says. "You're done for tonight. Go and get drunk, get laid. We'll see you tomorrow."

The first one leans in, dark skin glittering with a sheen of sweat. "But this is your virgin special. After this you take care of your own stiffs, you get me?"

I just nod, catch a glimpse of the dead guy's head smeared up the wall, his neck leaking ichor onto the white deck, half his face staring back at me with a blank eye, and I turn and puke again.

Michael. His name was Michael Privedi, he was a rat, and Vernon had me take care of it, because he thought I was a rat too. But I wasn't.

"We need to stop before I piss my pants," the girl says.

So she's wearing pants then. "You just want to run away."

"Fucking right I do!" she spits. "You're gonna get us both wasted! But out here in nothing but a T-shirt and panties? I'd be dead before morning. How about you stand beside me and hold my fucking hair while I squat? That work for you? I just need to piss."

She is so angry, and I can't blame her. But she's clearly terrified too. Not even twenty years old. Something jolts through me. Twenty years old. That's how old I was when I shot Michael in New Orleans. I don't know how, but I know I'm twenty-eight now. Why do I remember that and so little else? Eight years ago.

No wonder the car looks crappy. I pull over to the shoulder and get out, go around to her side and open the door. She looks at me and then tips her head towards my hands.

"I don't want to hold your hair. Just stay nearby."

She makes a hissing sound of disgust and moves a yard away to the edge of the trees. It's awkward for her to pull her underwear down with her hands bound up in front, but she does it, sits, and a stream of steaming piss hits the dirt. She really did need to go. It makes me want to go too, so I move away and piss into the trees with my back to her.

"You really know how to take a girl on a date, Eli," she says, and there's a tone of amusement in her voice, the anger a little dissipated.

I can't help laughing a little. "I bring all my girls to this stretch of highway for a piss."

She huffs, half a laugh, and I hear her scuffling around as I zip up. I expect her to be hightailing it into the woods as I turn back, but she's already back in her seat, pulling the car door closed. I get back into the driver's seat, start the engine, pull away again, the dark highway sliding by. As dark as my still empty mind.

"Where do you think we're going?" she says.

I don't even know her name. "North."

"North? How much further north can we go? There's nowhere you can go and outrun Vernon."

Michael leans through the gap between the front seats, one side of his head and half his face a ragged, bloody mess. "She's right, man. You know she's right."

I scream and the car swerves, gravel sprays from the tires. The girl slams her hands to the dashboard to brace herself. "What the fuck, Eli?"

My heart is hammering, my throat feels swollen with it. In

the rearview mirror, the back seat is empty. I twist around to see and there's no one there.

"The fuck is wrong with you?" She glances back too, smooth brow creased in a frown.

Man, she's beautiful. It's like I'm only just noticing that, but I've known it for a long time. I've known her since she was a child, ten years old, maybe less. As she got towards thirteen and fourteen, I hated myself for the carnal thoughts I had. Then she got to sixteen and seventeen, started looking like a grown woman, and everyone agreed she was a stunner. Long, black hair with a soft wave, startling green eyes, smooth skin. The body of a dancer and a heart-shaped face with full lips.

Her name rises up like a bubble through tar. Carly. Oh shit. Carly Sykes.

I've got Vernon's daughter.

"If you hadn't smashed my phone we could find out where the nearest motel is," she says after a few miles of silent driving.

"Motel?"

She looks at me, her gaze searing as I drive and I refuse to take my eyes off the road. "You were blanked out for a long time, Eli. You really scared me."

"How long?"

"You don't remember?"

"It's a little blurry." Understatement of a lifetime.

"Fucking *days*, man. You remember driving for two days with me in the trunk?"

I can't help looking at her and my shock must be written across my face, because her own hard gaze softens.

"You really don't, do you? You were like a zombie. You didn't even feed me for the first day and a half, or give me any water."

I lick my lips, shame burning my cheeks. "I'm sorry, Carly."

She shakes her head, stares down into her lap. I catch the glint of a tear reflecting the dashboard lights as it falls to her thigh, soaks into the dirty T-shirt. "I thought you were going to kill me too."

Who else did I kill?

"I guess there's a part of me that wouldn't blame you."

I remember I have a bag behind the passenger seat with a couple of changes of clothes, some cash, a few other survival bits and pieces. For whenever I found myself out on the road for a day or two, unexpectedly, sent on some mission for Vernon. I could maybe give Carly something else to wear from there. I get a flash of her standing in that oversized T-shirt, clean but shocked, the room around me drenched in blood. I gasp and my brain shuts down on the recollection.

"Hey! Hey, asshole!"

I blink and shake my head, turn to look at her.

"Don't you blank on me again, man. I need you to hold it together. I'm so hungry and so tired, and so fucking filthy. We have to rest. Find a motel, get ourselves sorted out. You stink, man. You need a shower too."

I let my eyes roam over my hands, realize I'm dirty as hell. There's dried blood on my pale knuckles, and jammed under my nails. A sidelong look at the rearview mirror shows my face is smeared with dirt like hers, more blood there too. Pretty sure none of it's mine. My green eyes are hooded, my dark, curly dark hair matted and greasy. I have a hell of a bruise across my right cheekbone, swollen and yellowing around the edges of a midnight blue lump.

"Okay." I know she's right. We've been driving like this two days? Surely there's enough space and time for me to catch up, figure shit out. "No names, no credit cards." The words come to me as easily as breathing. I know I'm good at this stuff.

"Like I've got those any more than I still have my phone." She leans back, gestures at herself with both hands. "Maybe I can at least get some fucking shoes?"

I grind my teeth. I have to stay in control of this. "No phone calls. You stay in the room."

Her eyes flash fury, she opens her mouth to speak. But I interrupt before she can get going.

"You give me your sizes, I'll get us both new clothes and whatever else we need. Meanwhile, I might have something here you can use."

She presses her lips together, staring daggers at me, but I keep my eyes on the road. Eventually she subsides, slumps back down into her seat, staring balefully out at the night.

Nothing more is said for over an hour and the whole time I'm searching the blank cavern of my brain, but all I come up against are dark walls. Except for one thing. My second kill.

Now, I know Vernon made me kill Michael Privedi. He was my first and made me puke. We'd come up together, Michael and me, both making good at Vern's heel. But Michael had always been a little unstable. I remember Vernon took me under his wing when I was eighteen, that memory is clear enough now. My parents died at the hands of a drunk driver when I was five, I remember that too. Well, I remember being told about it. In all honesty, I have precious few recollections of any kind until I was into my teens and in state care. I guess I've always had this propensity for lost memories. I recall hundreds of books though. Giant fantasy romps and science fiction space operas. Thrillers and mystery novels, Tarzan and Sherlock Holmes. I've been mocked my whole life for being a bookworm, but I'm a big guy too and learned early on how to fight, so I've never really taken too much shit off anyone. And I'd always retreat into books to hide from the pain of real life.

When I was fifteen or sixteen I used to skip out from school by hanging around in Privedi's Workshop with Michael. He'd skip classes too, his dad owned the garage. His old man didn't give a crap whether his son was in school or not, let us both hang around and talk shit with the mechanics, drink beer and smoke cigarettes while they fixed cars, or chopped them. When you think about it, Michael's dad was an asshole. But he was connected too, a wingman in Vernon's crew. And soon enough, Vern started showing an interest in me and Michael. Brought us both in when we turned eighteen, after grooming us for a good year or so.

Then only two years later, a jack mysteriously failed and dropped a '97 Buick right on Michael's dad. Except it was only a mystery to the police. We all knew Vernon made it happen because Mr. Privedi had been into the Colombian cartel for about fifty large and face had to be saved. The fool was playing around with all kinds of gamblers, and one of Vern's made men owing that kind of cash to the Colombians? Unforgivable. These memories are flooding back now.

But Michael couldn't forgive Vernon. He kept raving about how come Vern couldn't make some other retribution, save face some other way, why did his dad have to die? Michael knew the truth. He just didn't want to accept it. And so he started looking for a way out and that kingshit detective, Rob Bradon, got his claws in. Made Michael start giving stuff up. Of course, Vern had considered that possibility and was watching closely. As soon as Michael started to crack, Vern called a meeting at the house on Bourbon Street.

"I wanna make things right between you and me, about your dad," Vern had said to Michael.

Right then I started to get chills, I could tell something was up. So could Michael, he started looking left and right like a cat that's forgotten to check a room for exits. Vern's main wingmen, big black Charles and equally big, white and red-haired Peter, shifted up to either side of Michael and led him by the elbows.

"Let's go on the balcony for some air," Vern had said. "Eli, come on."

I'd started to tremble, wondering what the hell was up. Me and Michael, we were close like brothers, everyone knew that. If Michael had done something fucking stupid, was he going to take me down with him? At that point I'd no idea he was giving intel to Bradon, but I was getting concerned about him, wondering if he might do something unforgivable. I was so damn young and naïve then.

When we walked into that sticky night, out of the cooling comfort of the fans and AC, Vernon dabbed his sweating forehead with a white handkerchief and passed me a gun with the other hand. Now I can see him, square-faced, granite jaw, eyes a little too close together, dark and penetrating. Skin like cement, always a little bit grey. But he was strong and healthy too.

"We all know why we're here," he said, almost like he was too tired to even bother.

"You got this wrong, Vern," Michael said. His teeth were chattering like he was cold, and his eyes darted left and right, tears sitting on his lashes. "You know I wouldn't rat you out, you know I wouldn't cause you any grief, Vern. You know I'm not my old man."

Vernon shook his head. "Seems I know a lot of stuff. I'll

tell you the only thing I don't know." He looked at me and the weight of his gaze was like a punch.

The gun seemed to weigh a ton in my hand, but it was only a revolver. A thirty-two with six bullets. I already knew it would only spit one tonight. I had no choice.

Vern's face was blank. "I don't know whether it's just you, or you and your buddy here."

His eyes didn't leave mine, so I straightened up and met his gaze. I'd suspected Michael might crack, but I'd also ignored it, distanced myself a little since Mr. Privedi got flattened by a Buick, waiting to see how Michael would shape up. Self-preservation is a strong instinct. I had nothing to hide, nothing to be guilty about.

"I don't know what he's done wrong, Mr. Sykes. But whatever it is, it hasn't been with me."

Vern had smiled. "You only call me Mr. Sykes when you're nervous, Eli."

"Damn straight I'm fucking nervous now, Mr. Sykes."

"So prove to me you're not a rat. I know for a fact that he is. He dies tonight."

Michael had started gibbering and gabbling, crying and wiping at the snot flooding his top lip. Charles cuffed him into silence and he quietly hitched breaths while Vern stared at me.

"He dies tonight by your hand, to prove you're with me," Vern said. "Or he dies by Charles's hand and Peter kills you."

I shook my head, mind spinning, feeling like I was about to explode from the sheer pulse of nerves. "Mr. Sykes, I'm for you all the way, but please don't make me kill Michael. He's my friend. I've never killed a man before."

"It was bound to happen sometime."

"Sure, I figured that, but not my best friend."

Vern's eyes narrowed and a cold wave broke over me. "Your best friend?"

"Mr. Sykes. Vernon! I'm not a rat!"

And Michael's sobs grew louder.

Vern gestured to the gun hanging loose in my hand. "Prove it, Mr. Carver."

So I put that gun to Michael's ear and I pulled the trigger, before I could stop to think about it any more, because I knew I was a dead man otherwise. And I couldn't bear to hear another second of Michael's panic and distress.

And then I puked in a potted palm.

And Charles said to me, "But this is your virgin special. After this you take care of your own stiffs, you get me?"

Seems I remember more than I thought.

But that was my first kill. It is directly connected to my second. A guy called Alvin Crake who used to be a mechanic at Mr. Privedi's and talked a lot of shit about the man after Vernon dropped that Buick on him. Vernon had taken control of the workshop, of course, and technically Alvin worked for him. I used to spend a lot of time there still, the office out back was a place I conducted a lot of business for Vern. One day, after hearing just one line too much about Mr. Privedi and his shitheel son, I asked Alvin to join me in that office. He'd scowled at me, but came along. I'd closed the door behind him, turned around, and shot him in the face. I didn't puke that time, it was easy. I hated that guy. And I took care of my own stiff.

Told Vern that Alvin had been making trouble and the big man slapped me on the shoulder and said, "Well done for taking care of business. I never did trust that asshole." Which was fortunate for me. Then he'd gone about his day like nothing was out of the ordinary. I suppose it wasn't for him.

But that was another turning point for me. When I became a willing killer. There's been a few more since then, but they've all deserved it. Haven't they? I know there have been more, though I can't remember right now who they are or why they died. Everything's so goddamned hazy.

"Town up ahead," Carly says, leaning forward in her seat. "You have to stop, okay?"

"Yeah, okay."

A scattering of properties mark the start of the locality. Streetlights up ahead and then a sign saying PALM TREE MOTEL, 1 MILE. Carly looks at me pointedly and I nod. She's right, we badly need to rest and clean up. And we need food. My gut rumbles and I realize I'm starving. I've barely fed her, apparently. Maybe I've hardly fed myself either.

The sign for the motel is bright white and blue neon, glowing out over the dark road like a fake moon. I pull into the parking lot and brake to a halt, heart hammering. A police cruiser sits there on the asphalt, along with three or four other cars, presumably belonging to motel guests.

Carly shakes her head. "Don't you dare pull out again. We have to stop."

"Cops," I say stupidly.

"Yeah, no shit, cowboy. But we're not in trouble with the cops, remember? Quite the fucking opposite."

"But...look at us."

She holds up her hands. The cable ties have rubbed red raw lines into her skin, even made it bleed in places. "Maybe you should cut these off."

I lick my lips, look out the window. The motel office is lit up like a fish tank with venetian blinds on the inside and a cop has parted two with his fingers, stares out at us.

"Put your fucking hands down!"

I slap her hands into her lap and pull forward again, park across the lot from the cruiser and kill the engine.

"Let me preempt all your concerns," Carly says. "I'm not gonna run away because I'll be raped and killed by local rednecks before dawn running around like this. I'm not going to go to the police, because they'll ask way more questions than I can answer, and we both know Vernon has too many connections in the police anyway."

I frown at her. "You're not desperate to get back to Vernon? Surely turning me in is your best bet."

She frowns back at me, shakes her head. "I just need to be clean and get something to eat, Eli. Please. You cut these off, then I'll sit here like a good girl while you go and check us in. Then we'll go and take care of cleaning ourselves up."

"I'm looking pretty beat up myself," I say. "They might ask me questions."

"So tell 'em you got in a fight. Miles back, yesterday, whatever. What do they care?"

I take a deep breath, thinking of all the things that might get me hooked. I think the car is clean and legal. I'm pretty sure there's no contraband inside, nothing incriminating. But then, there's so much I don't remember, how the fuck do I know what's there? I've carried kilos of cocaine and weed and smack for Vernon before, so who's to say there's not a life sentence sitting in the trunk.

"Get moving!" Carly says. "I'm getting cold again."

With the engine off, the nighttime chill is biting down quickly.

"Okay."

Fucking cops, it's not like I've ever cared what they think before. I've had my run-ins with them often enough and they're all the same, looking out for themselves. Just as bent as the rest of us, except they do their crime from behind a badge and get paid by the fucking government for it.

There's a rush of warm air as I push open the office door and two people turn to look at me. A cop in front of the desk and an old man in a stained T-shirt behind it. The cop moves only a little to one side of the small space so I have to step right next to him to approach the old man. Bastard.

I give a nod and half a smile as the old man says, "I'm Clarence. Help ya?"

"Need a twin room, for me and my sister."

"No problem. Just tonight?"

"Yeah."

Clarence names a price and my heart thumps. I pat my jacket for my wallet, feel the square lump of it and hope there's money inside. When I open it up I'm relieved to see quite a few hundred. Good for a little while at least. I remember I have bank accounts. I have a vague memory of several stashes here and there too, cash tucked away. And other stuff, lot of little bolt holes. After what happened to Michael... After what I did to him, I've always been careful to have quick ways out.

"Sir, you okay?"

I snap back to the present, shake my head and the cop is staring hard into my eyes. He's got a sharp nose and pointed chin, looks like a giant fucking rat.

"Yeah, sorry. Just really tired. That's why I've stopped."

"You look a little worse for wear."

"Got in a fight. Yesterday. Outside a truck stop."

"That right?"

The best lies are the simple ones. The more complicated you make a lie, the bigger it gets, the more easily you trip over it. "Yeah. No big thing."

The cop nods, mouth twisted in thought. I hold his eye for a moment more, then turn back to the motel clerk, hand him the bills.

Clarence hands me a key with a ridiculously large wooden fob swinging off it. "You parked all the way over there outside number twelve, so you may as well take that room. It's a twin and we're quiet right now."

"Thanks."

I nod to him, then to the cop, and suddenly feel like an imbecile, waggling my fucking head around at everyone. Jesus, but I am tired. I could sleep right here on my feet. How long since I last slept? Something occurs to me and I turn back.

"Say, is there anywhere to get something to eat this late?" I don't even know how late it is, but spot a clock above the old man. Ten thirty-five. Not too bad.

"There's a diner one block down on the other side. It's called Noah's Place. There's a number in your room and they'll deliver for an extra ten bucks."

"Ten bucks for a single fucking block?"

The cop laughs and says, "Old Noah knows how to turn a profit. You're gonna pay it though, right? Save yourself a walk?"

I'm annoyed to admit he's right, but he is. "Ten fucking bucks. You should be over there arresting that thief instead of shooting shit here."

They both laugh and I grin at them, the tension in the air gone like it was never there. Maybe that didn't work out so badly.

I'm relieved to see Carly's silhouette still in the car as I trudge back across the parking lot. There's one tall halogen casting a pool of light into the middle of the lot, everything around it in blacks and greys, lost shadows. As I get near the disc of brightness, Alvin Crake falls into step beside me. His face has a half-inch-wide hole right between the eyebrows, the back of his head opened up like a bony flower blooming, the result of that casual shot in Privedi's office. I yelp, but swallow down panic as he says, "You'll never get away."

I suck fast, deep breaths in through my nose. I killed this fucker nearly eight years ago. He's not here. He can't be here.

He slaps my shoulder with one meaty palm and I feel it and hear the *thwack*. "You know it. You'll never get away. Vernon has too many connections, too many eyes, too many fucking people!"

I turn and swing a fist, aiming to crack him across his stupid square jaw, but my arm sweeps through air and there's no one there. Carly is looking at me with a frown through the passenger window. I glance back and that cop has his fingers in the blind again, watching me. I sweep my hand again, like I'm batting at a fucking moth or something, then swipe the other hand too. Have I overdone it now? Do I look more or less like a madman?

Carly pushes the door open, still frowning. "The fuck?"

"Don't worry about it."

"Where are we?"

I nod at number twelve, directly in front of the car.

"Good. Stay between me and the office, so they don't see I'm hardly fucking dressed."

I do as she says, it's a good idea. I hand her the key and she opens the door, goes inside. As I close the door behind me, she turns, holds her hands out. "I really want to wash. Please, cut these?"

With pursed lips, I look around. She's being okay with me, didn't try to run or scream at the cops. I guess I have to trust her. How much she's biding her time though, that's a mystery. Still, what can I do? I just need a knife.

"Use the one in your pocket." She's staring at my jeans.

Of course, I've always got a Swiss Army knife on me. The blade is sharp, bright and clean, shining silver. I slit the tie and she virtually sprints into the bathroom, slams the door and locks it.

A moment of panic passes over me, and I head back outside. The cop is gone from the window of the office, but the cruiser is still there. Our room is the last in the row, so it's easy to slip around the back and check. The bathroom window is tiny and barred. I hear the shower rushing inside. No way she's getting out of there, only way in or out is the front door.

I go back to the car and start searching the trunk. Nothing but some old oil stains. The back lights both have metal sheets bolted over the inside, to stop anyone in the trunk from punching out the light unit and waving out of the hole for help. If ever anyone throws you in the trunk of their car, that's the best thing to do. Wait until the car is moving, punch out the lights and wave frantically. Hope like hell someone sees you and calls the cops. So of course, people like me, who routinely put fuckers in the trunk, we make sure no one can do that. And that's probably why there's nothing else in here. If I had Carly there for a couple of days, I'd make sure she had nothing to use, no means of escape. Jesus, poor Carly, I feel bad for what I've done to her, but there must be good reason.

I get another wave of panic and rush back into the motel room. The shower is still going, the bathroom door shut. With a breath of relief, I pull the cord of the phone from the wall, rips the wires clean out. Clarence can bill me later if he wants to, but at least Carly can't call for help now. I should have thought of that right away. I'm so fucking tired.

I return to the car and get my bag from behind the seat. Clothes, toiletries, toothbrush, all that shit. The zip is open and there's a nine-millimeter automatic lying on the top. Just as well the cop never got a look at that, I don't expect it's legally mine. But good to know I'm armed.

As I head back to the room, the cop is returning to his cruiser. The rat-looking fucker raises one hand in a wave. "Take care now."

I nod. "You too."

I watch from the window, the room door closed and locked, as he backs up and pulls away into the night. The place is quiet and still except for the continuing rush of the shower. Then I realize I fucked up the phone before I called for some food. Goddamn it.

When Carly comes out of the bathroom, she's transformed. She seems taller, stronger than the beaten-down little girl in my beaten-up old car. Why am I driving that car anyway? I've had a dozen since I bought that from the chain-smoking woman who lost her husband and business in the same year. Something else to think about. I really did drink a bellyful of Lethe.

Carly has a towel wrapped around herself, her fine legs bare from the knees down. She is a stunning figure of a woman. Her hair is wet, hanging loose all around her face, laying over her firm shoulders. There's a muscular strength about her, she's not skinny, but not bullish either. Graceful. Lithe.

"I'm not putting that damn T-shirt on again."

I can't blame her for that. From my bag I take another T-shirt, hand it over. "I'll get you some better clothes soon, but right now all I have is my own stuff."

"And what are you, six two and two twenty pounds? Like anything is gonna fit me any better than that last shirt."

I dig around and find a pair of baggy track pants. "Can you roll these up or something?"

She shakes her head and takes the clothes back into the bathroom. A few minutes later she emerges with the track pants cut off at the ankle, rolled up at her hips and cinched tight. The T-shirt is pulled around and knotted at the waist.

"Your pants gave up their life for me," she says, eyes daring me to be annoyed.

I shrug. It's fair enough. She looks faintly ridiculous, but kinda hot too. All baggy like some eighties throwback. "You need some Reebok Pumps and a boom box."

She looks at me, one eyebrow raised. "You're feeling better, clearly. Making jokes now?"

I shrug again, because I really don't feel any better. Then again, before now I wasn't feeling anything at all. "The phone is broken, I have to go and order food at the office."

"I'm not going anywhere."

I take the phone and go to Clarence. He frowns at me as I walk in. "Some idiot ripped the phone cord clean out of the wall," I tell him.

"Damn thing was fine when I cleaned up in there this morning."

I put the phone on his desk, make a face like I don't know what to tell him. Honestly, I really don't. "I don't need a phone except to order food, so it's no big thing to me. If I can order from here?"

Clarence's face is dark as he pushes the office phone across the counter. He points to a menu tacked on the wall beside his laptop, Noah's Place. The number is big and bold right across the top. "Better hurry, he closes at eleven."

According to the clock, it's ten minutes to. I ring up and the kid on the other end sounds bored as hell as he takes my order for two burgers with everything, large fries with each, and a big bottle of soda. Tells me it'll be about fifteen minutes, so I tell him room twelve, and to make sure he knocks loud.

"Thanks, Clarence." I give the old man a smile and walk away, leaving our busted phone on his desk.

Carly is watching some late night chat show on the TV when I get back to the room. "I hope you ordered for ten people."

"I ordered enough."

She wrinkles her nose at me. "Seriously, go wash. You fucking reek."

As I get undressed, I realize my shirt is stiff with dried blood. Just as well it's black, so it only looks like dirt. And what must that cop have thought, me looking and smelling like this? The hot shower is like a benediction, washing away more than the dirt and blood. But it doesn't seem to wash in any more memories. When I push the shower curtain aside, step out into clouds of steam, a shape in the mist makes me jump, drop into a fighting stance.

"You've made a terrible fucking mistake, bro," Michael says. He's sitting on the closed toilet seat, half his face gone, smoking a cigarette like nothing's wrong. The sharp scent of the Marlboro is strong in the small bathroom.

"The fuck are you doing here, man?"

"Looking out for you. Aren't I the best example that you don't cross Vernon Sykes?"

"There have been many other examples, Michael. Some of them better than you."

"Well. Even still. You've made a big fucking mistake. And taking Carly?"

"You thinking about fuckin' that sweet thang?" Alvin says, leaning back against the sink.

Michael looks over at him with a frown. "What the fuck are you doing here, asshole?"

"Just tryin'a help."

I bark a laugh. "What fucking help are either of you two dead fuckers?"

"Seriously," Alvin says. "You're already in as much trouble with Vernon as you can possibly be. So fuck that hot bitch out there. I mean, man, she's fine. That body! And that mouth, tell me you don't wanna drive your cock into that sweet mouth."

I swing a punch at Alvin again, the second time I've tried to punch the same dead asshole in half an hour, but I only hit air and steam. I turn back to Michael, but he's gone too. A banging startles me, then I hear Carly opening the door, taking the food from the delivery boy.

"Hey," she calls out. "We need to pay this guy."

I pull on clean jeans and a T-shirt from my sports bag and go out to find my wallet and hand over the bills. I tip him heavily, wave him away and shut the door, then we both fall on the food like lions on a gazelle. I don't think anything has ever tasted so damn good.

Fatigue hits me like a truck once the food is devoured, my body finally admitting that I've been pushing too hard, for too long. All I want to do is sleep when I see Michael at the window, lifting the curtain aside to look out at the lot. A glance at Carly shows she's not seeing him, or choosing to ignore him. Given that there's no way she could ignore a guy with half a face who wasn't there five seconds ago, I can only assume I'm hallucinating.

Then Michael, still holding the curtain aside, looks around at me and says, "He's back."

Ice runs through my gut and I jump up, run to the window. Michael's not there by the time I've cleared the end of the bed, but I'm too preoccupied to care. The police cruiser *is* there, pulled up across the back of my car. The rat-faced fucker who tried to make conversation shines a flashlight out his window, checking out the plate. He nods and says something into his radio, then gets out.

"Get your shoes on."

Carly looks up from the bed, where she's laying flat out and almost asleep. "What?"

"Shoes, now. Grab the bag. We're leaving."

"What the fuck, Eli, I need to…"

"Now!" I yell and it's like my voice physically lifts her to her feet, because she's standing by the bed, reaching for the bag in an instant.

"I don't have any fucking shoes," she says, tears in her eyes. She looks really spooked again, watching me like a cow watches the farmer with a bolt gun in his hand.

I pull on my boots as the cop slowly approaches our door. Carly comes to stand beside me and I stuff my hand into the top of the bag and pull out the automatic.

"What the fuck, Eli?"

She seems to be asking me that a lot. I push her back behind me and say, "This is gonna be messy."

"Who is it?"

"Cops."

Her voice is a strained and panicked whisper. "You're gonna waste some cops?"

"Just one. No choice." Then I look at her, one last glimmer of hope fading as I ask, "They can't help us, right?"

"Of course not."

I move to the side of the door, looking out the small window beside it. The cop is on the sidewalk right outside.

"Vern would get us anywhere," Carly says. "But especially in police custody. We can't trust cops any more than strangers."

That last hope stutters out and as the rat-faced cop reaches up to knock on the door I put the muzzle of the automatic against the weak plywood and fire three times. He staggers backwards, his chest and throat bursting out bright crimson in the weak glow of that tall halogen over the parking lot. I pull open the door, but he's already dead, staring at the dark sky. Steam is curling from the police cruiser's tailpipe, so I grab Carly by the arm and haul her along. We jump over the dead cop and into the cruiser, then I'm flooring it, the tires spraying gravel as we fishtail out of the lot and onto the main road.

Adrenaline has slammed my fatigue away for now, my focus tight, my vision sharper than a bird of prey. Carly is muttering and sobbing and clutching her knees again. The police radio is crackling, then a voice comes over, but I can't make out the words for the blood pounding in my ears. In the mirror I see movement in the back seat, behind the cage, and bite down a gasp. Michael and Alvin are both there, twisting around to see out the back window.

"That old man Clarence is on his knees out there," Michael says.

"Old fucker is howlin' like a whipped dog!" Alvin says, laughing like that's the funniest thing he's ever seen.

"They can trace this car easy."

Carly's voice cuts through my pulse and the voices of those dead fuckers. "What?"

"The police. They can trace their own cars. GPS and shit. We gotta dump it."

She's right. I nod tightly, looking around. The town is small, the streetlights far apart. Most everything else is dark, but for a few shops with illuminated window displays. The place is a ghost town. Noah's Place shoots by on the right, all closed up and dark but for its neon sign.

"Jesus, Eli, you're in some shit here. You ever wasted cops before?"

I look over, wondering how much to tell her. Because I don't fucking know. I'm sure I've killed plenty more than Michael and Alvin, but any cops? Any real people? I just don't know. My hands are shaking on the wheel so I grip it tighter before she can see.

She jabs a thumb back over her shoulder. "I mean, you left your car right there. He made it, obviously. Tell me it's not in your real name, Eli."

I swallow, thinking hard. I bought that car so long ago, but I don't think I've used it in years. That skinny woman with the broken life and narrow cigarettes, she wanted cash. I didn't even register the damn thing when I bought it. Maybe it's still in her name.

Oh wait, I used it in a job that went bad. I remember now. Had to get away fast, ran right into a cop standing on the corner outside the bar. He had his gun leveled at the car, squeezed off one shot, then I swerved and clipped him. Didn't kill him, I remember that, sent him sprawling and he came up onto his knees, holding one arm against his chest like it was broken, his face twisted in pain. And I bolted, managed to not get followed, and I took the car to Vernon's place. It had stolen plates over the real ones on it for that job, Vern kept an eye on things and, after a few days, announced that neither we or the car had been made, but best not to drive it around any more. He said to leave it on his property, he had someone come out and fix the ding in the wing and the bullet hole in the hood, get rid of the fake plates. Then he let his teenage kids drive it around for fun. No wonder it's so beat up, it's been a private joy ride for six or seven years.

And that was my third kill.

Not the cop, but in the bar right before. Vern had sent me to whack a guy by the name of Sylvester Barclay. Sly Barclay. He was a small-time hood, worked for the Jamaicans. I guess he was Jamaican too, I don't know. But there was some balance to be redressed. One of our boys got killed in a drug deal with those guys that went bad, and Vernon told me we had to even the slate.

"We gotta waste one of theirs," he said. "Go down to Maloney's and see if that Sly Barclay is there. I know him and some pals drink there all the time."

"And bring him in?" I'd asked.

Vernon laughed. "Fuck no, son. Put a bullet between his fucking eyes. Public execution. And say, 'We're even now.' And walk out."

Bold as brass and twice as hard, that's how Vernon liked to do business. So I put on a balaclava, walked into Maloney's and there was Sly right there. But he was already standing, had a gun pointed right at the door. Somehow, someone inside had tipped him off. I hit the deck and rolled as the place burst into crazy mayhem. Sly had three others with him and they started moving, fanning out to find me and finish me. I was alone, it couldn't have been worse. Thankfully, the regular patrons all panicked and ran or hit the deck themselves, so the only feet moving towards me were Sly's goons. From the floor I shot under the table and took out two of them at the knees. They went down screaming and I leapt up and rolled, made the gap behind the bar. There was a barman crouched down there, reaching for a shotgun. Without pause I swung my gun butt into his jaw and he dropped like a sack of rocks. I grabbed the shotgun and came up pumping. That was the first time I got shot, Sly fucking Barclay put a bullet in my shoulder then I put a hole right through his torso. His other buddy was about to lean over the bar looking for me and I leveled the gun at him. He rose up, real slow like he was underwater.

"I only came for Barclay," I told him, muffled by my balaclava and because my teeth were gritted in pain. My shoulder felt like it was on fire. "Let's not make this worse." Then I remembered Vernon's orders. "We're even now."

The two mooks on the floor, still howling in pain and clutching their ruined knees, were not dead, at least. I hoped the Jamaicans would accept the situation and call it even. Surely they didn't want a war. The one at the bar nodded, dropped his piece and backed away. I kept the shotgun sweeping the room, trying not to get dizzy at the pain, ignoring the blood soaking into the sleeve of my jacket.

My car was outside, and I jumped in, but that cop must have heard the shooting and was creeping up the sidewalk. He squeezed off a shot, I knocked him down, and then I was out of there. I've still got the scar from that bullet wound, but Vernon's in-house doc pulled the slug, stitched me up neat.

All of which means the car has been out of action for years, so I must have taken it from Vernon's place when I went on the run. Did I run from Vernon's? Is that where I got Carly? And what was that cop looking for? Whatever, it was enough to make him come knocking to ask questions. Maybe I could have talked my way out, no big deal. Perhaps I just fucked up back there, but it's too late to worry about it now. What's done is done.

"You coming back?"

I suck in a long breath again, realize I'd been phased out for a while. The street's dark, we've driven right out of town and onto country roads again.

"I'm here."

"You haven't been for the last twenty minutes. You gotta stop doing that, Eli."

At least it wasn't two days this time. "I'm here now."

"So what are we gonna do about this car?"

As we round a bend onto a straight, two pinpoint red taillights appear in front, a few hundred yards ahead. I accelerate and catch up, see it's a small Toyota, pretty non-descript, decent condition. A quick scan of the dashboard and I find the switch, blip the lights and sirens. A woman's face, lit up red and blue, appears wide-eyed in the rearview mirror of the Toyota. She indicates, pulls over.

"I suppose that'll do it," Carly says.

"Bring the bag."

We get out and I go straight to the driver's door, haul it open and drag the woman out. She's screaming and thrashing, but I throw her away, make her stumble across the road well out of reach, then get in. My knees crack the steering wheel and I grab the bar, scoot the seat back. Carly's already in the passenger side, my bag on her knees. Our doors slam almost simultaneously and I'm accelerating away.

"Neat and easy," Carly says.

"For now. This'll be reported stolen in no time."

"Yeah, but at least it can't be traced like the cruiser. We need to find something else, but we can make some distance first."

I'm so confused by what's happening here. I just wasted a cop because I'm clearly on the run, but why isn't Carly against me?

"You're being very helpful."

She laughs, shakes her head. "I want to stay alive."

"I'm not going to hurt you."

"Any more? I know that. At least, I think I know that now."

She seems so small and vulnerable. "Why aren't you mad at me?"

She laughs again, but it's bitter. "Oh, I'm mad as fucking hell, Eli. You hurt me, you scared me, you kept me in the fucking trunk for two days. But there's more happening here, right?"

"Is there?"

She looks over, then leans forward to look more closely. "Do you remember?"

My gut clenches. Is it really that obvious? "Remember what?"

"Oh man, she got you now!"

I press my lips together at the sight of Sly Barclay in the back seat. His dark face is all shadows in the mirror, but his eyes are bright. I know if I could see lower, there'd be a gaping hole where his chest should be. I catch his eye and shake my head.

"Oh yeah, she got you, man. She knows you faking all o' this shit."

Michael leans in from Sly's left. "It's true. You gotta remember, dude. But what might happen if you do?"

"What might happen, motherfucker?" Alvin says from Sly's other side.

The rat-faced cop leans in. How the fuck do they all fit back there? His name badge glitters in the dim dashboard light and I see OFFICER GRANEY stitched above it. There's a wet, dripping hole where his throat should be. "What might happen, Mr. Carver?" he asks, his voice gravelly and harsh. How does he know my fucking name?

The four of them rock back in the seat and laugh, their eyes and teeth white in the darkness, blood bright red all over them.

The space they occupy is like a cave, an uncannily wide seat with room for them all, and I can see it all in the mirror every time I glimpse away from the road, space contorted out of true to accommodate them.

"Eli?" Carly's eyes are wide too, but in concern, her full lips downturned. She's dropping into fear again, the flashes of confidence she'd been starting to show washing away like dust in a rainstorm.

"I've always got an out," Carly says. "If I did escape from you, I could spin any yarn I like to Vernon and he'd believe it. He saw you take me. But it's not that simple. I can see a chance here, though I'm starting to doubt it."

What is she talking about? A chance for what? I stare at the road, searching my memories. It's all black once more, my head as empty as the night ahead of us.

"Do you remember?" she asks again.

I breathe deep and even, steadying my nerves like I do on a job, controlling the adrenaline that's starting to surge.

"Eli? About Caitlyn?"

And something electric pulses through me, heaving up though I try to press it down, but it's unstoppable and her face swims into my mind. Caitlyn, with her blue eyes and copper red hair. Caitlyn with her musical laugh and furious Scottish temper.

Caitlyn Carver.

My wife.

She wasn't in the life until I brought her in and even then, I did my best to keep her out of it. That was always going to be dangerous, but Vernon was obliging.

"You're like a son to me," he said. "You watch her and I'll let it lie."

The implicit threat was clear, but I knew I could handle things. My god, Caitlyn was beautiful, and powerful, and funny. I saw her first only about a year after the botched Sly Barclay job. But not so botched after all, so Vernon had decided. Despite the additional two kneecappings, the Jamaicans had called it even, things had gone back to normal there for a while. Vernon told me I'd done well under trying circumstances and that was to be applauded.

"Adapt and survive, son, that's the mark of a great man."

So he thought I was a great man? I swelled with pride and let that small compliment fuel me for months. And maybe that's why I was so filled with confidence that day when I went into Maloney's about a year later. It was still called Maloney's even though old Maloney himself had sold and moved on after I'd knocked him out with a gun butt. He knew the place was getting too popular with made men and other gangsters, he wanted no part of that. Fair enough. So of course, Vernon bought it and used it as one of his many legitimate fronts. We didn't do much business there, but I liked to go in for social reasons. Have a few beers with the guys, play pool, sometimes watch a band. Maloney's had a good stage up the back and a decent sound system. After Vernon took over it started to develop a reputation as a good blues joint and the weekends got extra busy. They had to take on new staff and one of the new girls was Caitlyn Lansing.

I went swaggering into the place one Friday night feeling like a fucking giant for no particular reason, except maybe Vernon thought I was a great man. Or maybe simply because it was the site of one of my proudest moments, even though I'd originally thought the whole thing a debacle. I went up to the bar and this stunning redhead smiled at me and we locked eyes. Copper hair and blue eyes is a rare combination, so I'm told. It mesmerized me for a moment. She grinned, knowing she'd bowled me over, and that grin seemed to say that in this case she didn't mind at all.

"New girl?" I asked.

"Aye, started last week. You regular?"

"I am, but I have a feeling I'm going to be a lot more regular from now on."

She laughed, that magical music, and then the band had hit the opening strains of a twelve-bar beat and talking became difficult. I pointed to the pump, she smiled and pulled me a beer. We made plenty of eye contact for the rest of the night, I didn't hang around the bar like a loser but went to watch the band, hung out with some pals, but every time I needed another beer I'd wait until she was between customers and pin her with my gaze. She'd lift a glass, I'd give her a thumbs up, and she'd pour. Right off the bat, we just got along.

I wanted her so much, but I felt something else there too. Something beyond desire, maybe even something spiritual. I agonized over whether or not I'd stay until closing, try to take her home. Then decided to play the long game.

As the band took a break, I put my empty beer glass on the bar. She raised a fresh one, lips split in a sweet smile, and I shook my head. "I gotta jet, sorry."

"Aw, I was hoping you'd stick around." She twisted to look at the clock above the bar, her fine body on display in tight jeans and white tee. "I get off in a little under two hours."

My blood pulsed, but I knew I didn't want to fuck this up, so I gave her my most winning smile and said, "I would love nothing more, really. But business is pressing. You on tomorrow?"

"Sure am. Will I see you?"

"Most definitely." And I walked out, my cock heavy in my jeans, partly unable to believe what I'd done. But it felt like the right decision. I went home and masturbated furiously and had to drink a flask of whiskey to sleep, despite the beers.

The next night I went back, not too early so as not to seem desperate, I showed up a little after ten and she lit up when she saw me.

"You weren't lying!"

"I was not. And tonight I plan to stick around until you get off. When's that?"

"Hopefully about an hour or so after you take me home?"

And that was it. We fucked all that night and I'd never experienced anything hotter in my life. Of course, Vernon knew all about it within a couple of days. He called me into his office at the estate and asked me about her.

"She's special, boss. Really."

He nodded. "Well, she works for me, but in a legit capacity. You keep her away from our business and it's all good."

"You got it, Vern. No problem."

"It might be better if she didn't work for me," he said, one eyebrow arched.

I knew he was right. Distance was essential. "Don't sack her. Not yet. I'll sort it out."

It took a few weeks, but she was talking about going back to school, she wanted to be a real estate agent but could never afford the courses. I convinced her I could afford it, she should quit the bar, move in with me, go to school. We were so hot for each other, fell in love hard and fast right away, and never shied away from telling each other so. It was perfect. She knew my income wasn't entirely above board, but that was as far as she chose to pursue it. She was happy to accept the things I wouldn't tell her, and I assured her there was nothing really bad involved.

"You don't, like, kill people, do you?" she'd asked, laughing nervously, uncertain.

I laughed right back. "No, baby! Nothing like that!"

It was the only time I ever directly lied to her. As she slowly got her first qualifications and then a job as an assistant realtor downtown, she also came around a little more to the idea of what I did. It's funny how people ease into the life gently, and after a few years they don't balk at stuff that would have horrified them before.

She would come to Vern's estate sometimes, for the big social events. She knew Vernon Sykes was my boss, but never asked in too much detail about what I did for him. The estate parties were always fantastic fun, barbeques and drinks and playing in the huge pool. It was at one of Vernon's parties, right after I turned twenty-five, almost two years to the day since we'd met, that Caitlyn told me she was pregnant. Man, I went over the moon, we were going to be a family.

Vernon's parties.

Where's Caitlyn now?

Pregnant, right after I turned twenty-five. That was three years ago.

"Eli? Eli, don't you fucking blank on me!"

Vernon's parties.

Red washes over my eyes, I see four tiny limbs all pointing in the same direction.

Darkness closes in on the red.

The road ahead is awash with wan light, a peach and grey dawn rising through the trees to the right. Darkness like indigo ink to the left. A girl is in the passenger seat, sobbing quietly. She has a dark bruise around one eye, a cut just above the eyebrow that's dried up, started to scab over. She's wearing track pants and a T-shirt that are both way too big for her, the pants cut off at the bottom of the legs. Her knees are drawn up to her chest, arms clutched around them, her feet are bare. She has her face pressed to her knees, muffling her weeping. Her black hair hangs like a shroud over her head.

Carly.

It's Carly Sykes, Vernon's daughter.

Something stutters deep inside me, I remember a different car, a motel, gunfire.

Fuck, I shot a cop. We took the cruiser, then a Toyota. The badge in the middle of this steering wheel isn't a Toyota logo. We're in a different car, but I don't remember switching.

It was night, now the dawn is rising. I must have blanked out for a few hours.

"How long?" My voice is low and gritty, like morning voice when you haven't spoken for hours.

Her head snaps up, tears standing in her red raw eyes. "You're fucking back, you piece of shit?"

"How long? A few hours? It's nearly morning."

"A few hours? Fuck you, Eli. Fuck. You."

I take a deep breath. "How long?"

"Today is Saturday, Eli. You shot that cop on Thursday night. You remember murdering a fucking cop?"

"Yeah, I remember that." Something nags at the side of my brain, like a dog scratching at a screen door to get in. Something about red, and small people. Nausea ripples across my gut and I push that thought away. I can't let that in again yet, I think that might be where I went last time. I owe Carly better.

"What else happened?"

She sighs, tips her head back against the headrest. "I'll give you the short version. You went dark on me again. I'm not bringing up what we talked about, but you gotta get your shit together, man. This is first time you've said a single word since then. We drove for hours in that stolen Toyota, then as the sun came up you found a truck stop. You parked, and just left. Went inside. There was some shouting, some crashes like breaking plates and glasses. I thought about taking the car and clearing out, right there and then, and I really should have, Eli." She starts crying again, tears rolling over her cheeks. "I really fucking should have, I don't know why I'm still here. Maybe it's some kind of fucking guilt, though God knows none of this is my fault. None of it!" she yells, then breaks down sobbing again.

I give her a minute, then ask, "What happened?"

She sniffs, drags a forearm across her face, takes a shuddering breath. "You came back out with handfuls of fucking cash. Like about three grand or something. You handed it to me and then you drove on. We got to another town and you parked outside a used car dealership and just sat there waiting. So I took the money inside and I bought us this car. Because I figured that's probably what you wanted. I let the guy see down this baggy-ass T-shirt and I batted my eyes and I got the car no questions asked. Signed fake names without him asking for ID or anything, because he was a sleazy fucker. You sat outside in that Toyota. So I drove away in the new car. And you followed. Once we got out of town, you flashed your lights, I pulled over, and you took over driving, just left the Toyota sitting there. I asked you something and you did this, you asshole." She points to her eye, her cut brow.

"I did that?"

She doesn't say anything, just glares.

"What did you ask me?"

"I'm not fucking telling you, man. You are unstable."

"I'm really sorry, Carly. I don't know why I did that. I can't imagine doing it now. I…I wasn't myself, I guess."

"That's no fucking excuse!"

"No, it's not. But it is the reason. I'm sorry."

We lapse into silence again. We're in a legit car at last, bought for cash, not hot. With any luck the cops won't zero in on that dealership any time soon, which means we're mostly under the radar again. Maybe we can stay that way and I won't have to kill any more of them.

"Where the fuck are we?" We've been driving for days, half of them I can't even remember.

Carly doesn't take her eyes off the road ahead. I can't blame her for not wanting to look at me. "Somewhere west of Philadelphia. You've been avoiding cities, passing around shitbox towns, sometimes driving in circles."

Where do I think I'm going? Away from Vernon Sykes, sure. But with his daughter kidnapped, am I just trying to get away or is there some kind of plan? My brain feels like high country desert, cold and barren, full of dust and pretty much fuck all else.

"We have to stop, Eli. You need to get your shit together."

"Yeah. I do."

The back seat of the car is half lit by the rising dawn. Shadows shift and move there, but I'm expecting them this time. I wait to see what smartass things they've got to say. Nothing helpful, I'm sure.

Michael leans forward first. "It all started with me, huh? Can you remember your life before you fucking killed me? Before you wasted your brother from another mother?"

"You made that happen," I tell him. "You're the rat."

Carly frowns at me. "What?"

Michael laughs. "Like I had a choice!"

"You always were a fuckin' weak little shit," Alvin Crake says, leaning right close to Michael's broken face. I can see the bony flower at the back of Alvin's head catching the first rays of the morning sun. "You an' your dad were both shitheels an' deserved to die."

Michael wheels around on him, snarling, and they tumble backwards in a mess of thrashing limbs, rolling through that uncannily large space that makes the back of the car.

Smoke swirls up, weed, the aroma thick and cloying suddenly in the enclosed space. "So they no help," Sly Barclay says, then draws heavily on the thick joint. His face disappears in a cloud of smoke as he exhales, but I still hear him. "What you gonna do, man? Where you think you're going?"

Officer Graney leans in, takes the joint from Sly and sucks deeply. A smile spreads across his face and smoke roils out of the hole that is his ragged throat. "You're going down, Eli. One way or another. We'll get you, or Vern will. Or we'll get you and *then* Vern will." He smiles, hands the joint back to Sly. "That's good stuff."

The smoke is drifting all around Carly and me. She doesn't seem to notice, stares at me with confused eyes. But I can taste it, feel the effects of it pushing a little more cotton wool into my brain. The last thing I need now is to be stoned.

"Give me a hit on that." A skinny, pale face appears between Sly and Graney and they shift over, make room for him.

Who the fuck is this?

"You need a plan, *cocheeese*." The southern drawl in his voice is strong.

Now I remember this racist sack of shit. It's the weed that's brought him back. We used to buy off him and his redneck idiot friends, transport it to dealers in the cities: Atlanta, Birmingham, Knoxville, Charlotte, Nashville. That was one of my regular jobs, to pick up big vacuum-packed bricks of weed from this asshole and drive them to one of those places, make the second deal and deliver the cash to Vern's banker. Easy money.

Except this racist asshole always rubbed me up the wrong way. Dwight Ramsey. Yeah, that's right. Fucking Dwight. And then Dwight gets in a little trouble trying to rip people off, starts thinking he's a big player, not some shithead grower, and Vernon says to me, "I think our friend Mr. Ramsey has outlived his usefulness."

I didn't need any more instruction than that and drove right down into the swamps west of Jacksonville that very night. For a bunch of fucking idiots, Dwight's operation was pretty tight, but he was so used to me his goons opened the gate and I drove up the hill to his place without any trouble. I parked outside his wooden house and he came out onto the veranda and lifted a beer can in greeting.

"Hey, cocheese, can you believe what that fucking nigger in the White House done now?" he asked, like we were right in the middle of a conversation.

I still had one foot in the car when I raised my automatic and put a slug right between his eyes. I've always been a crack shot, no idea where I learned to be such a good shooter, but it's always served me well. I've always felt like I was a natural, Vernon said I was born to it. But I practiced diligently too, still do. Natural talent is only the start, the rest is continuous hard work.

I was back in the car before Dwight's corpse hit the deck and back down the hill before his people even knew what happened.

I waved as I drove through the gate and his goons frowned at me, must have realized right then something was up because they turned tail and started sprinting back to the house.

"What the fuck do you know about anything?" I ask.

"Are you talking to me?" Carly says. "Eli, the fuck is going on here?"

"I know plenty, cocheese."

He always called me that, one of so many things about him that just pissed me off.

"Like, I know you ain't ever gonna outrun Vernon Sykes. He's got a hunnerd guys just like you, all of 'em fucking better than you, and they'll soon *do* to you what you did to me. 'Less you think you can get out of the country. You reckon you can do that, cocheese? Days on end drivin' around and around aren't going to help. When was the last time you slept?" He jabs the joint at Carly. "She's been getting a few hours here and there while you drove, but you ain't. What's it been? Four days without a wink? Five? You're losin' your fucking mind, cocheese."

He leans back, hands the joint to Sly who takes a big hit. "Racist fuckwit here is right, man."

"You have to sleep," Graney says, taking the joint from Sly. "You have to sleep and get your head together. You need a plan."

They're right. They keep passing that joint around, the smoke getting thicker and thicker, filling the car like storm clouds. It's sweet and strong and my mind is swimming and I can't see.

The car swerves and Carly is yelling at me, grabbing the wheel. "Wake up! Pull the fuck over before you kill us! Wake up, Eli!"

I manage to get the car to the curb and she jumps out, runs around to open the driver's door. She pushes at me. "Get over. Sit there, wind the seat back and sleep. I'll keep driving, okay?

I'll just drive us around and I'll only stop for gas and I'll pay cash. You sit there and sleep, Eli, please."

I can hardly see her, let alone argue. She leans over me, I feel her breasts against my chest as she struggles with something, then the seat is tipping into the back and I go with it and all I want to do is sleep forever.

It's dark when I wake up, every part of my body aches. I open my mouth and it's dry as a lizard's ass. Carly glances over from the driver's seat.

"Finally! Here." She hands me an open can of Coke.

It's a little warm, but does wonderful things to my mouth. I wind the seat up and look out, see trees going by, ghostly in the headlights, long empty road ahead. Seems like it's been a long empty road ahead forever.

"Epic sleeping."

I rub my eyes. "How long?"

"About fourteen hours straight. I stopped for gas about two hours ago, otherwise I've just been cruising, going nowhere. Parked up a few times and just looked at the view."

"Where are we?"

"Somewhere west of Martinsburg, I think. I had to circle around or we'd be going to fucking Canada."

I remember something that racist Dwight said. "Might not be such a bad idea. Get out of the country."

"Depends how much they know about you killing that cop. Bound to be cameras at the motel." She looks over, her eyes worried. "They must know you killed him, Eli. If you want to leave the country you'd only manage it with the help of someone like Vernon. You know any other Vernons?"

"Kinda, but maybe not well enough to ask for that kind of help." I start to think about it, all the ID men I know. Maybe

I could organize something, though it might be hard to do without Vernon finding out. My head is clearer than it's been in days, but I still need time and space to think about this stuff.

"We need to hole up somewhere and figure shit out," Carly says. "We can't just keep driving aimlessly around."

"Why are you helping me? I kidnapped you and you've had ample chance to run."

She looks over, nervous, then back at the road.

"What?"

She frowns, lips tight. Then, "I'm scared of saying anything to you. Scared of what I might trigger. You hurt me when you blank."

"All the more reason to get the fuck out, no?"

She laughs bitterly. "Yeah, maybe it is."

We lapse into silence again as the night darkens further around us, the last of the indigo leaving the sky behind.

"Seriously though, you should be turning me in." And even as I say it, I know there's been something else there all along. Something that's made me okay with trusting her, but that I'm not letting myself think about too much. "I mean, you're his daughter."

She looks at me, horrified, her eyes flashing fury. "I was never his fucking daughter! He married my mom when I was a kid, that's all. And when I turned eighteen he killed her to have me."

"He killed her? Had you?" Memories swim like sharks in the blackness of my empty head. They're stirring down there, agitated, about ready to come surging up to feed.

Carly clams up, stares at the road.

"Tell me, Carly."

"I'm scared you'll go under again."

"I won't."

"You can't promise me that! You can't stop it."

I sigh, shake my head. "That's true. But I have to know, Carly."

She drives in silence for a while, then, "You think that hit-and-run was really random? My mom taken out like an annoying mole, excised from Vern's life so neatly, so he could have me? She died, and he made it clear he would look after me. He also made it clear I wasn't a little girl any more. He took me whether I wanted it or not, had done for years anyway. You lot all knew and didn't do a thing."

The memories swim upwards, snapping their teeth. She's right. We all turned a blind eye, let Vernon replace his wife with his wife's daughter, because what could we do? "I never thought he killed her," I say, and I'm not lying. "I remember him taking you as his new wife after she died, I thought that was creepy, but it never occurred to me he had your mom killed for that."

"You naïve fucking idiot." Tears are on her lashes again, but they don't fall, tethered there by her rage.

"Yeah. I guess so. How long ago?" My brain is skidding without purchase, trying to place events.

"Two years."

"So you're twenty now?"

She glances across again, brow creased. There's something else here, something she's not telling me. Something massive.

"Why didn't you leave him?"

"Oh, like it's that easy?" She's really hurting inside, using anger as a shield. "He controlled everything about our lives, Eli! Everything. My mother had no agency at all, so I sure as hell had none. After he killed her and took me I had literally nothing. He's had me under his wing me since I was eight years old. He's been fucking me since I was thirteen. I've got no money, never had any ID, nothing."

"I'm sorry." She's been in an effective jail all this time. I imagine her running away anyway, even being on the streets is better than what she's describing. But is it really? She'd still be raped, no doubt, probably killed. At least with Vernon she had a roof, food, all the toys she wanted. It was prison, but she's right, what else could she possibly do?

"Oh, you're sorry? Now? You know what, you're a far better guy when you can't remember shit. You're a far more decent fucking guy right now than you've ever been before." I open my mouth to say something, I don't know what, but she plows right on. "I couldn't believe it when you took me after… After what happened." Memories surge and gnash their teeth and I force them down. Not yet. She looks over at me, checks I'm still engaged, I guess, not blanking on her again. She sniffs, still angry, but refusing to cry. "I suddenly thought maybe this was a chance I'd never imagined before. After all that horrible shit happening so suddenly, maybe something good would come of it, for me. You'd have to run and hide, and you had me with you. I thought it was my out. You'd take me along, protect me, at least for a little while, until I found a new life, got some money. But I didn't expect you to start blanking out. To tie me up and throw me in the fucking trunk, Eli! To kill cops. But despite all that, I still thought maybe there's a chance. Is there? Eli? Is there?"

No wonder she's helping me, trying to stay with me. Maybe I did kidnap her, but if I took her away from Vernon's enforced life of rape and helplessness, perhaps she's right and there is a way out with me. And like she said before, she can still turn back at any time, turn me in to Vernon, go back to that life. It's better than death or destitution.

"You still think I can help you." It's not a question, seems like such a dumb, pointless thing to say. Her desperation claws at me, drags at my heart. But those other recollections are swarming and churning down there in the dark.

She sighs heavily. "Maybe."

"If I can only get my shit together, right?"

"Right. Can you?"

"I'm trying."

We pass a large billboard advertising Green Hills Motel, 2 Miles. She points at it. "That's gonna be our new home for a little while. We gotta stop driving around."

"Okay."

"And when we get there I'm going to tell you something. And you have to do your fucking best not to blank out on me again."

"Okay."

"Maybe start trying to brace yourself or something."

"I'll try."

They're all lined up in the back seat. Alvin, Sly, Michael, Dwight and Officer Graney, shoulder to shoulder, grinning at me. Another joint is traveling slowly back and forth.

"This is gonna be good," Alvin says.

"I'll bet you twenty he cracks and goes bananas," Dwight says.

Michael looks at me hard. "Brother, you've got one chance. You think hard and you make it work, okay?"

Sly's laughing, shaking his head.

"We'll get you first," Graney says, wagging one index finger. "Oh, we'll get you, some PD, somewhere. And shall we hand you over to Vernon? Hmm? Maybe!"

Alvin cackles, rubs his hands together. "Oh man, he's gonna lose it! I reckon he won't blank this time, he'll go ballistic instead. That right, Eli? Do it for me! Fuck that li'l bitch. Fuck her in every hole she's got, then kill her an' fuck her again."

"Jesus, man." Sly's looking at Alvin like the man is literally made of shit, and he's not far wrong.

"What do you think?" Graney says. "You going to rape and kill her? Or just kill her? Who else are you going to kill? Maybe some more cops will come to this motel and you'll kill them too. You're just racking up the life sentences, boy. We'll get you."

"One chance," Michael says, squeezing my shoulder so hard that his fingertips dig in and make me wince.

"I don't think you'll survive much longer, cocheese," Dwight says. He snorts, hocks up something brown and sticky, tobacco distending his cheek. He spits on the ground, then looks back up at me. "I hope a fucking nigger kills you. The most undignified death. You deserve nothing less."

Sly leans forward in the seat. "You got a problem with me, redneck?"

"You a nigger, ain't ya? Course I got a fuckin' problem with you. Subhuman piece of shit."

Sly launches right across Alvin's lap and starts raining punches down on Dwight's face. I see Dwight's nose burst in a shower of blood, and Alvin's leaning back clapping his hands and laughing like a hyena. Officer Graney leans away from one side, shaking his head. Michael catches my eye again. "One chance, brother. Hold. It. Together."

"Here it is," Carly says, and the tires crunch gravel as we pull into the lot.

The motel is green and cream, surrounded on three sides by tall trees, a few spotlights in the parking lot cast pools of light. We get out of the car and walk together towards the office. I look Carly up and down, suddenly see she's wearing jeans and a T-shirt that fit, a short leather jacket and bright new sneakers.

She grins crookedly. "Yeah, so when I stopped for gas it was in a small town and there was a store right opposite. You were sleeping so hard, I couldn't wake you, so I locked you in the car and bought clothes. I used some of that money you stole from the truck stop. Where you'll also be on security footage, by the way."

I frown at her.

"I was only in the store for five or ten minutes! You slept right through it, didn't notice a thing. I couldn't go any more without clothes or shoes, man."

"No, no. That's fine, of course. I'm thinking about the footage you're talking about. Might be there's my face all over TV and whatever, from the cop thing at the motel, the robbery at the truck stop. My face must be everywhere, right?"

She purses her lips. "Yeah, you're probably right. It's been a couple days, easily enough time for people to start taking notice, watching out for the cop killer on the run. Maybe you should stop shaving. Get some bleach for your hair."

"You still have some cash on you?"

"Yeah."

"Then you book us in. I'll wait in the car."

"I'll be on CCTV too, from the motel, at least."

"I guess we'll have to chance it. You've done a lot less than me. Here." I hand her a trucker's cap from the back and she pulls it low over her eyebrows.

I sit in the shadows of the car and watch her in the office, chatting and laughing. There's an old woman behind the counter with a face more wrinkled than my ball sack, but she's all smiles and open body language. Looks like Carly is charming the shit out of her.

The motel is two-story and Carly secures us a room upstairs on the end of the row. I'd rather be on the ground floor, but it'll do. Can't expect her to know stuff like that. I'll have to school her a little. When we unlock the door and walk in, they're all lined up on one of the beds: Michael, Alvin, Sly, Dwight and Officer Graney. They're grinning like idiots.

"Oh, we ain't gonna miss this show!" Alvin says, his eyes alive with excitement.

Along with the bullet hole between his eyes, Dwight's face is puffy with bruises, his lip split, his nose bleeding. Sly really beat the shit out of him. They're at opposite ends of the bed, but seem to have settled their differences for now. Dwight is grinning, showing off bloody teeth. Sly is casually smoking another reefer, smiling crookedly, his eyes hooded, smoke curling out of the huge ragged hole in his chest. Organs hang in there, glistening and pulsing. Graney wags that index finger again and Michael raises a finger of his own. Yeah, one chance, I know. I need to not lose it here. Not let the blanking thing happen and not let these circling memories eat me alive. I'm more than a little scared, I feel like a child. Something throbs in my gut at that thought and I bite it down.

Michael is serious-faced, his voice little more than a whisper. "Hold it together, brother."

Carly takes my gun from the bag and holds it loosely in her hand while she shuts the door. "Go sit over there." She points to the bed with all those dead bastards lined up along it.

I look from her back to the bed, start to gesture and say it's occupied, but it's empty now. There's muffled sniggering and they're all in the bathroom, crowding around each other to look at us through the door. All in various states of entertained, except Michael, still serious as hell.

Carly has one hand on the front door handle, the other holding my gun. "We really have to get focused here, okay?"

I sit on the bed, as far across the room from her as I can be, clench my hands together in my lap. "Okay."

"I'm going to say a name. You have to try to focus. It's gonna hurt like hell, but you gotta get your shit together, Eli Carver."

I take a deep breath. "Okay."

She frowns, purses her lips. Then she takes a deep breath of her own and says, "Caitlyn."

My body shudders. Beautiful red hair and glittering blue eyes. Oh man, my wonderful Caitlyn. Red starts to swamp my vision, Carly receding into it like a car powering away along a foggy highway.

"Hold it together!" Carly shouts, and she's crying again. "Please, stay with me. You have to *face* this!"

I grind my teeth, biting down on a howl that wants to burst out of me and split the night wide open.

"I'm going to say more, but don't you lose it, Eli! Don't make me shoot you and have to go back to him!"

"Tell me," I growl, but it's already coming up anyway, unbidden like irrepressible vomit, impossible to hold back.

"My birthday party," Carly says, sobbing openly now. "And Caitlyn. And Scottie."

And my brain explodes in fire and hate and fury.

Vernon's place is huge, a sprawling estate with the main house like something from a fairy tale, all towers and gables and crenelated edges. Several other buildings are dotted around the grounds and pools, with a stepped lawn out back that can hold a thousand summer barbecue goers and still seem spacious. But those events were always business. Carly's birthday was just family. And by family, that meant the closest members of the crew too, so I was there with *my* family.

Vern had been drinking, which was not all that common for him. A big deal had gone south, he had the DEA on his ass, people were being killed. Business was at a low, but that happened from time to time. I guess that's why he took the excuse of the party to have a drink, but it never did sit well with him. Lots of others had been drinking too. Carly's twentieth birthday, for some reason, seemed to bring out the rager in half the crew and their partners, and by eight in the evening people were raucous. Except Carly herself. She spent the whole afternoon and early part of the night looking stressed and put out. I couldn't figure why. Vernon had bought her the most amazing diamond necklace thing, and there was a new Corvette on the gravel drive that had to be worth a mint. When he'd handed her the keys she had just shaken her head. "Maybe later," she said, and Vern grimaced, his left eye twitching.

I knew that sign. We all did. When Vern's left eye started to go, someone was going to get it. So the crew were a little on edge, but most of the partners had no idea. And the drink kept flowing and the edges began to round off. Or so I thought. But it turned out Vern was still pissed.

Carly made it clear she was at the party under duress. She made it equally clear she kinda hated her husband right then, when usually she was quiet and resigned about it. Of course I knew the whole thing was a fucking mess, Vernon marrying her less than a year after her mother died. He was more than thirty years her senior and there'd never been anything between them beyond a strained stepfather to reluctant stepdaughter thing. But then they'd got married, she'd seemed glassy-eyed during the ceremony, but accepting, and we all just went along with it the same as she did. You don't cross the boss, after all.

Except Caitlyn. Oh, Caitlyn, why couldn't you have just sucked it up like everyone else? Like even Carly did. But Caitlyn was adamant that she would show her disgust. Maybe she knew about the rapes since Carly was thirteen. Perhaps the women talked about that stuff. But I kept my word to Vern and kept Caitlyn as much at a distance from the business as I could. Of course, family stuff was different.

And by around nine o'clock on the night of the party, Carly must have decided she'd put on enough of a show. She disappeared for a few minutes, I suppose none of us thought anything of it. Bathroom break or something. Then she came back wearing a long T-shirt like a nightgown, and nothing else, bare feet, hair down, face defiant.

"The fuck is this?" Vernon asked.

"I'm going to bed."

The air thickened, tension building from a strange root of rebellion.

"It's early," Vernon said. "You can't leave your own party yet!"

"I can," Carly said, lips twitching like she was trying to not cry. "I'm tired, it's been a big, exciting day." Then she'd cast a look at him that was saturated in hate. "I want to be well rested so I can drive my new Corvette tomorrow. Did you buy me lessons too?"

We all knew the car was more of a symbol than anything else, but she could have driven it all over Vernon's sixty acres.

Vern wasn't having it, and he'd been drinking, was uncharacteristically drunk. Unusually stressed. His regular shield of iron control was crooked and he backhanded Carly across the cheek. So sudden and unexpected, despite anything else we might have suspected, we'd never seen him hit her before. The room froze, kind of a thick silence filling the place up like water. Carly looked at him, eyes wide, tears rolling over her cheeks and a single trickle of red tracking from one corner of her mouth. She just stared at him.

Eventually Vernon said, "Don't sass me, you little bitch. Go and get dressed." And he raised his hand to hit her again.

Carly just thrust her chin forward, daring him to do it. No one else in the room moved a muscle, and then Caitlyn said, so quietly, "Don't you dare." Her Scottish accent was soft, but always in evidence. It was a beautiful sound. But right then it was strong and menacing.

She was right beside me and I put a hand on her arm, opened my mouth to tell her to quiet down, not her business, when she looked at me and said, "Don't you dare, either. Not one of you fuckers."

"Pardon me?" Vernon's voice was ice cold.

"You all stand here and don't raise a word to defend her, let alone a hand," Caitlyn said, eyes scanning the room. "And you, you fucker." She pointed at Vernon. The silence became almost solid, tension in the air like molasses. "Bad enough you hold her here and fuck her whether she likes it or not. You don't get to hit her too."

Caitlyn had been swallowing a few drinks of her own, that's all I can think of to explain why she suddenly felt she could challenge Vernon like that. He turned to her, one hand in the pocket of his expensive linen jacket, the other still half raised where he had been going to hit Carly for the second time. Carly's eyes flicked between Caitlyn and Vernon and there was something in there, something lost and pleading.

"Pardon me?" Vernon said again.

"You fucking heard me."

I put a hand out, took Caitlyn's forearm and I wasn't gentle, tried to turn her towards me. "That's enough," I said, but it's all I got out before she shook me off.

She pushed me away from her, eyes furious, red hair flashing in the chandelier light like fire. "Oh, that is not fucking enough. That is not nearly enough. Bad enough that your business is whatever it is, but at least here, with these people, you should show some respect to each other."

"Five seconds to rein your bitch in," Vernon said to me, his voice level.

I stepped towards her. "Caitlyn, please, we need to go now. This isn't—"

"Fuck you!" she screamed at me. "You can't all stand around here and let this happen to Carly. Why are none of you fuckers standing up for her? Against this fucking rapist piece of…"

And Vernon showed her why no one did. His hand came out of the jacket pocket holding a nine millimeter and I yelled and dove towards Caitlyn, but Vern was quick and nearly as good a shot as me. *Bang! Bang! Bang!* And three red spots in a triangle dead center of her chest. She staggered back, blood bubbling as she opened her mouth to scream, but it was a gargle. And she dropped. That was it. Gone. Dead.

My mind started spinning, others in the room were backing away, Carly had her hands over her mouth, sobbing, eyes wide. Vernon turned his gaze back to me, the gun still in his hand. "I warned you on day one she was trouble. I am not best pleased I had to take care of that trouble myself."

Fury roiled in me, my muscles spasmed in a kind of tautness that paralyzed me. I wanted to kill him, I wanted to wrap my hands around his throat and squeeze until his fucking eyes burst. And he saw that in me. He tipped his head to one side, eyebrows high.

"Yeah, Eli? Really? You wanna run at me? Have a fucking go, I dare you."

And then movement in the doorway far to my left. Strawberry blond hair from his mom, curls from me. He had my green eyes and broad face and shoulders. Scottie, my rough-and-tumble little bruiser. Just over two years old, we'd celebrated his party here only two months before. "What's the noises?" he asked, rubbing puffy eyes, woken from the silk sofa in the room next door where we'd put him down hours before, peaked on sugary cake and excitement.

And Vernon had looked at him, then back at me, his eyes red from drink and rage. "I think our relationship is at an end, no?" Vernon said.

And I started to mouth something, some words, I don't know what. My mouth opened, my body shook, and all I managed was, "No, no, no."

And Vernon fired. One shot. Scottie's chest turned red and he flew back through the door he'd just entered by, all four limbs pointing back accusingly at Vernon Sykes. His tiny, round face and equally round mouth, an O of utter surprise as he vanished from sight.

And I was moving, and Carly was screaming, and crew members were running, grabbing partners, some trying to get out, others trying to get between Vernon and me. I had a knife in my hand and I opened the throat of Pauly Brand and he collapsed in a waterfall of red, staring at me in disbelief. Then my hand found my own nine millimeter and I started firing, left and right, almost randomly, but I'm a good shot. My mind was lost in a scarlet haze of grief and raging fury and all I wanted to do was kill everybody, destroy everything.

I can't remember how it all went down, but I know there

was slaughter. And then I found myself momentarily still and Carly had run in front of me, Vernon was ducked behind a huge mahogany cabinet full of awful porcelain statuary and Carly was screaming, "Stop it! Stop it!"

And several guns were on me. I was well outnumbered, by skilled men, and though I'd killed a few, I never had a chance. I froze and Vernon reappeared, face twisted in rage.

"Fuck me, Eli. What a mess."

He wasn't wrong. And I was a dead man standing. Unless…

I grabbed Carly and slammed her back against my chest before anyone could move, pressed my gun against her temple. I count bullets subconsciously, it's a habit we all have, and we all knew I had two left. And another clip in my pocket.

"Nobody move!" Vern yelled.

I backed out of the room, Vernon staring at me and I could tell he was deciding whether or not to sacrifice Carly to have me, but there must be something real inside him after all, because he paused.

"I'll fucking kill you," he said, and I continued back, didn't answer.

I had no chance to get away, not really. Vern's estate was huge, he had guards everywhere, it would only be moments before they had the jump on me again. Except right outside the front door was the old car I'd bought off the skinny woman with the hand-rolled cigarettes all that time ago. The one the teens used for joyrides around the estate. Right there with the keys in it. We were in and gone in seconds, slewing left and right on the gravel driveway as I powered dangerously fast for the gates. They were closing automatically, an order from the house, but I squeezed through, the metalwork on one side squealing as sparks flew, and I was out. I needed to grab one of my emergency bags. I kept a few around the place, with a change of clothes, stuff like that. I sped a mile down the road, then grabbed a cable tie from my pocket, bound up Carly's wrists and threw her in the trunk. She was screaming and yelling at me, but I was already shutting down, already blanking out. I needed her for security, couldn't risk her running away, I had no idea what I was going to do, and then I was driving again and my brain locked down and down and down and everything went dark.

"Eli! Please, Eli!"

Carly is pressed back against the door, trembling all over, crying. My gun in her hand is wavering, tracking left and right over me as I sit on the bed, my muscles locked tight all over as the incandescent fury blisters through me. Blackness creeps in and pulses out at the edges of my vision, my heart is pounding.

"Eli, come back! I *need* you!"

Carly's voice is like an anchor, hauling against me every time I try to let the black take me. I don't want to remember. I don't want to see little Scottie flying back from the room, so surprised. I don't want to see that triangle of red spots appear on Caitlyn's chest. I can't live with that. I can't live with the guilt, the knowledge that my life led to theirs and their lives led to that. Blackness swallows and Carly screams.

The five fuckers are lined up near the bathroom door, all leaning forward, like they're expecting me to actually explode. Officer Graney, neck and chest blood-soaked, is wagging his finger again. Dwight and Alvin are laughing, almost dancing a jig.

"Cocheese gonna go apeshit!" Dwight says.

Sly is grinning, sucking on a reefer the size of a Cuban cigar, it's cloying stink filling the room. "You deserve all o' this, you fuck."

And Michael, shaking his head, turning it further one side to show me the blown-out skull and teeth, the ragged wet hole where his ear should be. Like he's reminding me what I did, what Vernon made me do. Like he's telling me, "You expected anything less after this? You thought you were fucking special somehow?"

And their presence has anchored me little further, ironically given me a moment to hold the blackness away.

Carly is leaning forward, the gun hanging at her thigh. "You back, Eli? You with me?"

I draw a ragged breath, look up to meet her eyes.

"Oh, Jesus," she says. "Are you really? You're really still here?"

And I'm sobbing like a child, my chest heaving, my face flooded with tears and snot. "They're dead," I manage between gasps. "They're both dead."

Carly nods, tears of her own spilling but she's still not game to come near me. The hand without the gun reaches out, like she wants to hold me, console me, but I'm a caged tiger and she's not putting her hand between these bars, not yet.

"Jesus fucking kee-rist," Dwight says. "The fucker is crying!"

"You weak fucking shitweasel," Alvin says, his face twisted in disgust. "Don't cry! Fuckin' rape this bitch, then kill this bitch, then go and kill Vernon!"

And part of me wants to. Part of me wants to do nothing but hurt and kill and desecrate everyone I've ever known because my Caitlyn and my little Scottie have been torn away from me and the world is fucked. There is nothing good, nothing wholesome in the life of humans. We're broken fucking animals, eating each other alive, and I want to stand atop a pile of bones and blood, and scream my fucking defiance at the heavens, and then spill my own life out at my feet and let the blackness take me forever.

"Yeah, fucker, that's more like it!" Alvin says.

Dwight's dancing again. "Hoo-ee, now you're acting like a man!"

"One chance," Michael says and his voice is calm enough to make me look him in the eye. "You break now, you're broken forever," he says. "This is it. One chance."

"Please, Eli," Carly says. "Come on. Hang in there. We can do something."

"Do what?" I manage to growl, and Dwight and Alvin exchange a look of disgust.

"We can finish this," Carly says.

I turn my gaze to her, drag breath in through my nose, fast and shallow, my heart hammering a pulse in my throat I can almost taste.

"Finish it?"

She nods, holding my eyes with her own, still streaming tears, but intense. Focused. "Vernon lost men in that deal, he's got the feds on him, his shit is messed up. You took out Pauly and Kirk and Peter. Maybe others. I know for sure Charles survived, but no idea who else. It's been a few days, but Vern's weakened, right? If you give him time to recover, to gather a new crew, you'll never get near him. And once he's found balance again, he'll come for you and you'll never get away. I'll have to go back to him, to protect myself, I'll have to and I won't be able to help you. But now, if we move quickly, we can move against *him*. Kill the shit-eating motherfucker. Let some other crews fill whatever gaps we leave and then we'll both be free and clear."

And I realize she's right. I can never outrun him, I'll always be watching my back. My other crimes, Officer Graney, the truck stop, notwithstanding, I'll never outrun Vernon Sykes. And I can't live anyway, not without my Caitlyn and Scottie, not while

Vernon is still breathing too. All I can do is take him out. Or die trying. Carly says she'll help. She's scared, maybe she'll turn me in to save herself anyway, but what other choice do I have?

"So how do we do it?" I ask, and the blackness has receded from my vision. My gut is a seething lava pit of grief and anger, but maybe it can fuel me, not consume me.

I look over at the bathroom and all five are standing there, looking disappointed. Except Michael. He simply looks resigned, and he nods once.

"You're swaying where you sit," Carly says. "Lie down. Sleep again, let your brain settle. We're safe here."

"Safe?" But I think she's right, for now at least. I fall onto my side, pull my feet up. Grief chews holes through me, I can't get their faces out of my mind. I roll over, turn my face to the wall and let the pain come again. I hear the other bed creak as Carly sits while I quietly sob and at some point a new blackness steals in and I sleep, deep and dreamless.

TWO

I WAKE TO TOTAL BLACKNESS and the sound of soft snoring behind me. I'm still facing the wall, haven't moved a muscle in hours and my body aches like I've been beaten up. My knees pop as I stretch and slowly sit up, my head pounds.

They're really gone.

The tearing grief is a ragged hole in me, sucking away light and goodness, hauling against me like a vortex, but it's somehow dulled. Maybe I'm too broken down to feel it like before. Maybe it's just not possible to feel that wrenching pain continuously and survive. My mind is closing doors here and there, blocking up corridors of thought to protect me. But one is wide open. One has a light at the end, and it's the face of Vernon fucking Sykes. I remember him as I last saw him, watching me back out of that door, Carly pressed against me. He was scowling, narrow-eyed, hate and murder in that gaze. But there was some resigned loss, too. Maybe, just maybe, the breakdown of his deal, the trouble he was in, the loss of control at Carly's party, all in such quick succession, made him see his empire crumbling. Perhaps Carly is right and if we move fast enough he might be ruined enough that we can finish him.

I walk to the bathroom, feet silent on the cheap motel carpet, and don't turn on the light until I'm inside and the door is shut. Cold water on my face washes away some of the pain and some of the fogginess. Helps me find some sharper focus. Who will I have to get through?

Carly said I killed Peter, that big red-headed bastard. I remember dropping Pauly with the knife, but he was only ever a runner, a bootlicker. She said I dropped Kirk as well, so that's a bonus. He was a fucking psychopath and too dangerous for even Vernon to keep too close by, but he was loyal as a dog. I'm glad he's out of the picture. Short of a handful of regular guys that Vern can call in, it's only big Charles with his shiny bald head and ebony skin I have to worry about. And Vern himself, of course. So if I know Vernon Sykes, and I do know him well, he will have gone to ground somewhere, keeping Charles right at his shoulder. He'll be gathering whatever men and resources he can, trying to rebuild. I need to figure out where he's gone to ground, take him and Charles before they regain that strength of numbers.

"You think it's going to be as easy as finding him?" Michael says behind me.

They're all there, lined up in the mirror.

I shake my head. Of course it's not as simple as that, but I have to start there.

"You gonna have to shake down a whole bunch of people, cocheese" Dwight says. "Start liftin' rocks and shouting at cockroaches, see if you can't find information."

"People ain't gonna give up information easy," Alvin says.

"And as soon as you ask," Officer Graney puts in, "word will get back to Vernon very quickly that you're asking around. How will you stop him from being one step ahead all the way?"

"Why the hell are you all helping me?" I ask, watching their faces float in the mirror.

Sly holds out a joint, like he's offering it to me.

"We all buddies now, all of a sudden?"

Sly laughs, shakes his head. "We just wan' see you try, motherfucker. And die horribly for your efforts."

I suppose that makes a kind of sense.

There's a light tap on the door.

"Who are you taking to?" Carly asks, her voice small and frightened.

I turn and open the door. The five amigos are nowhere to be seen. "Just myself."

"You still here? Still okay?"

"Not okay, no."

She looks down, unable to hold my eye. "Yeah, sorry. But not blanking. You're talking, so that's a good sign, whether it's to yourself or anyone else."

"I didn't talk before?"

"Not when you blanked, no. You'd go hard, like a statue. It was terrifying. And you hit me if I didn't comply, whether I understood or not."

Now it's my turn to look down. "I'm sorry."

She puts a finger under my chin, lifts my face gently. "You really are, huh?"

"I know I'm not a good guy. I've done more than questionable things, but I've always had some kind of code. I've always tried to do right by people. Not hitting women has been high on that list. I should have done more to protect you from Vernon. Omission is still guilt, I guess. I'm not proud of that."

She frowns. "You're a better guy now than I've ever known you before. Code or not, you were a hardass, nasty piece of work all the time you worked for Vern. This... Well, I guess it's no surprise it's changed you."

"I feel like all my shields and shells have shattered. When I had Caitlyn and Scottie, for the first time ever I felt like I had a life to look forward to. We even talked, Caitlyn and me, about getting out of the life. Moving somewhere, me getting a regular job. We were gonna have more kids, were already trying." A sharp, barbed hook hitches in my chest. "And he took all that away."

She squeezes my hand, just nods, lost for words. We stand like that for a moment, then I say. "So where do we start?"

"It's the middle of the night."

"So?"

She turns and goes back to the bed, falls flat on her back staring at the ceiling. Her eyes glitter in the soft light from a red LED bedside clock that reads 3:04. "Vernon will have gone to ground."

I sit on the other bed, elbows on my knees, staring at my hands hanging above the hard-wearing carpet, almost lost in shadow. "I was thinking the same thing. Do you know how bad it was with the deal that went south right before your birthday?"

She's still staring at the ceiling, like maybe there are answers up there. "Worse than any of us realized, I'm guessing. I think that's why he went so...so uncharacteristically..."

I nod, still watching my hands as I pick at my fingernails. Grief is welling up again, a tide that threatens to swallow me whole. "Yeah, he was obviously stretched far beyond taut. He was using your birthday as an excuse to forget about things for a while."

"He hardly ever drinks, and never that much. I watched him sinking bourbon after bourbon and I wondered why. I know it made me push harder than I might have otherwise."

I look up, but she's still staring above into nowhere. "You poked the bear while he was vulnerable?"

Her gaze snaps to me. "Don't try to make this my fault!"

"I'm not, that's not what I mean. But it contributed. And then Caitlyn." I hitch a breath, her name like a blade in my throat. "Then Caitlyn really pushed too hard and he snapped."

"Any one of those things might have passed without too much drama. But all together…"

"Yeah. So the deal that went bad. What do you know?"

"You don't know?"

"I'd been on another job, hadn't been in for a few days. Your party was my first time back at Vern's for nearly a week, I was planning to catch up the next day."

She settles back, looking up at the ceiling again. "Well, I don't know much. You know how it is, I was the plaything at home, never in on the business. But I heard plenty, always tried to stay informed where I could, in case it was ever useful. And because my life was fucking boring otherwise. Anyway, the details are beyond me, but the big picture is this. Vernon had a deal set up for a lot of cocaine. It was coming from some Colombians, but Vern refused to deal directly with them. Some bullshit about one of the main guys there having disrespected him once before."

I sigh. "He's done that before. Uses intermediaries to make the other party feel like losers, not important enough to deal with Big Vern himself."

"That's it. But the intermediary he uses this time is in trouble. Charles and Peter were in charge, but that Tweezer guy was making the collection and dropping the cash."

"The biker? Seriously, Vern put a Desert Ghost nobody in charge of a deal like that?"

"No, he put Charles and Peter in charge, but told them to use Tweezer. He thought it was funny, having this wasted, grizzled old biker turn up with the cash and leave with the cases of coke."

"So what happened?"

"Tweezer had no idea, but he had a police tail. Had it for a couple of weeks apparently. He'd run some guns over from Texas two weeks before, made a deal that nearly got him picked up, so he'd aborted the run. The police assumed he still had the guns and was laying low, waiting to make the delivery at a later date, so they were watching. They see him heading off with a big case, in a car instead of on his bike."

I'm nodding, hands rubbing slowly together as I see it take shape. "So the cops think he's making another run at delivering the guns?"

"Right. Except he's still putting that off for the time being and fulfilling his little job for Charles and Peter in the meantime, completely unaware that he's surveilled."

"What a fucking idiot. If the original gun deal went bad, he should have known the cops would be watching."

Carly laughs softly. "Sure. But this is Tweezer we're talking about."

"Right. And the deal gets busted?"

"Yep. A couple of Colombians die in the gunfight, Tweezer took a hit in the leg, apparently, whether from the cops or the Colombians I don't know, but it makes no real difference. Charles and Peter got away, obviously."

Now I can see the whole picture. "So the deal is busted, the money and the drugs are in police custody, as is Tweezer, and Vernon doesn't know whether the fucking loser will squeal or not."

"Exactly. As soon as the DEA realize what they've stumbled onto they start following leads. So of course, Vernon gets a call. 'Anything you want to tell us?' they ask him. 'Go fuck yourself, talk to my lawyer,' says Vernon. But that's where it stands. So when my party came around, Vernon was stressed, unsure how much the Feds knew, unsure how likely Tweezer is to cave."

I let a soft laugh out, shake my head. "He'll fold up like a tissue paper house in a tornado. I can't imagine how many priors he's got, but regardless, they've got him dead to rights on this deal. If he takes it on his own, he's solely responsible for what I imagine is a big amount of coke. That's a life sentence, right?"

"Almost certainly."

"He'll definitely cut a deal."

Carly sits up, crosses her legs atop the mattress. "However!"

I raise an eyebrow, smile. "There's a twist?"

"Kinda. Naturally Vernon isn't taking any chances. He wants Tweezer dead. So he organizes a hit in the hope he's soon enough to get Tweezer before he blabs. The morning of my party, he hears that the hit went bad and Tweezer is still alive in there, still liable to talk."

"So surely Vernon organizes another hit right away?"

"And *that's* what he was waiting on at my party. That's why he was drinking. The longer it takes to kill Tweezer, the more likely it is that Tweezer will crack and get Vernon in the shit. He still hadn't heard yet when everything went…you know. Meanwhile, Vern's lawyers are working overtime, shoring up against any chance of Tweezer saying something that'll stick."

I sit there staring at my hands again, breathing deeply and slowly through my nose. This is good. Talking and planning like this, it stops me thinking too much about Caitlyn and Scottie. Maybe if we keep talking, I might get their dead faces out of my mind for at least a few moments at a time. "So that's where we start," I say eventually.

"Where?"

"Find out if Tweezer went toes up or not. And either way, find out who's been contracted with that hit. Whoever that is will have a way to let Vernon know the state of play, so if we find the hitman, we might find where Vernon is hiding out."

"*If* Vernon is hiding out," Carly says.

"If?"

"Yeah. I mean, if the hit was successful and Tweezer died before fingering Vernon, then the cops have nothing on him and he can go back to business as usual."

"Which is gathering his remaining crew and coming after me?"

"I assume so. Coming after me, more specifically, with a plan to kill you. I'm abducted, don't forget."

"Yeah. Right."

"And that depends on whether Vernon has managed to get people around him again. It might take a while, so maybe we still have a few days, maybe not. But if Tweezer is still alive, then Vernon is almost certainly in some shit right now and will still be laying low." Carly raises both palms up, shrugs. "Right now we have no idea about any of it. We can't know anything beyond the state of play at my birthday. After that, it's all dark."

"How long has it been?" All those blanked out moments, those periods where I shut down, did horrible things to Carly. How much might Vernon have accomplished while I floundered?

"My birthday was Saturday. It's nearly Sunday now."

I'm stunned, silent for a moment, then, "A week."

"Yeah."

"So Vernon has had a week to get organized."

She nods, lips pursed. "If Tweezer is dead, we might be in trouble. But if the hit hasn't been made, Vern may still be struggling."

"Or of the hit was successful, but Tweezer had already given up some dirt," I say. "We may find that Vernon is fighting off the DEA right now."

"We can only hope."

Another thought strikes me. "Or if Tweezer is dead, but Vernon is still weak for manpower, he might still be laying low anyway, regathering his strength."

"Maybe."

"We need to know and not waste any more time."

She gives me a sarcastic *You think?* look.

I stand up, pace back and forth as I try to figure out a plan. "So if we need info on all of this, that means we need to know what state Tweezer is in. And what he may or may not have said before finding himself in said state. Which means we have to find a way to chat to some Desert Ghosts."

Carly twists her mouth in disdain. "Fucking biker gangs. Great."

"But first, we need to not look like us. The car we have is safe for now. How attached are you to your long hair?"

"Seriously, you want me to cut it all off?"

"And bleach it? How do you fancy a peroxide pixie cut?"

She laughs, shakes her head. "Guess I'm game to try it. And you?"

"I've got a week's worth of stubble here. I'll shave my head and maybe cut this into a goatee. Reckon that'll make us both look different enough to casual observers?"

"What choice do we have?"

"Okay. I'm going shopping. You'll stay here?"

She gives me a crooked smile. "Still so convinced I'm going to run out on you."

"I guess the life makes a man paranoid."

She moves to sit next to me, puts one hand on my knee. "Everything here is beyond fucked up, Eli. But I know you'll do what you can and I know I'm only going to be safe from Vernon when he's a fucking corpse. So yeah, I'll stay here. I'll help you. If it goes really bad, I'll tell anyone who will listen that everything happened against my will. You abducted me, you made me do stuff. And I'll have to go back to Vern and maybe I'll get another chance to get away. I won't lie to you, I'll drop you like a hot rock if I have to. But I don't want to and I will help you all I can."

"I appreciate the honesty." I'm not lying. Truth like this is worth far more than some line of bullshit and she's smart enough to know that.

She just nods.

"So I'm going shopping."

"You can't wait till morning?"

"Quieter now. There'll be somewhere open."

Without a backward glance I pull on my cap and drag out an old hooded top from my bag, pull the hood up over the cap and make sure the peak is down low. If I hunch my shoulders, keep my face in shadow, I should be okay.

I find an all-night pharmacy not too far from the motel and the walk through dark and quiet streets has done me good. Given me time to think. But I try not to think of too much. I'm pretty sure I'm not going to blank again, but every time the memories rise up, I choose to push them aside. I won't bury them again, where they can eat me from down deep. But I won't think too hard on them either. The images, red blooms, tiny limbs, are burned into my mind like brands on a steer, but I won't look right at them, won't obsess over them. I need to focus here and two things will keep me on track. One is the sure need that Vernon Sykes needs to die. The other is that I have to protect Carly and make it as right for her as I can. There is a chance for her here. Maybe I can see some tiny bit of atonement in giving her back her life. I'll let the grief out after that.

The woman behind the counter in the pharmacy is nervous when I put the stuff on the counter. I can't blame her, really. I'm not looking up much, avoiding all the CCTV cameras, shoving cash at her with grunts and gestures. I've bought the most suspicious things possible, really. Peroxide, razors, scissors. So I've added a toothbrush and paste for Carly, and grab some gum from the little display on the desk.

She rings it all in. "This everything?"

"Yeah."

There's a pause and I wonder for a moment if she's going to try to be a hero. Tell me she needs the manager, or she just needs to make a call or something. I'm tense as hell, and my hand creeps around to my back where the gun is jammed in the waistband of my jeans. I don't want to shoot anyone else. Ever. Except Vernon Sykes. I want to shoot that fucker until there's nothing left of him.

I can tell the clerk is looking at me, trying to decide something. Don't do it, lady.

She draws a deep breath. "You okay, honey?"

"What?"

"You okay? You hurt? You need help?"

Jesus fuck, she's a good Samaritan. "Fine. Really tired."

"That's all?"

"Just finished a double shift."

"Okay, honey."

I slide money over the counter and she lets her fingers linger on mine as she takes it. "I'm here all night, don't finish until eight a.m. If you decide you need anything... Even if it's only to talk."

I grab the paper bag and nod. "Thanks."

I can't stop thinking about her all the way back to the motel. What a bizarre world this is, really.

Carly is fast asleep in bed, an inviting line of curves under the covers as she lays on her side. I creep around the room, bemused that she can sleep through my return. I know I'd wake if I was in a strange room and someone came in, even if I was expecting them back. I guess that's the difference in our lives though. She's always been safe except from her captor and there's nothing she can do about that. Her long, even breaths trigger a wave of fatigue over me and I know I'm ready to crash too. I hope I don't dream. Once the room is locked up and a straight-backed chair from the little desk in one corner is jammed up under the door handle, I shower, piss, and fall into bed. Blackness swallows me like a whale.

I wake up to the sound of running water. The room is bright, curtains wide letting in the day. It doesn't feel early. My body protests when I push myself up on one elbow. The clock beside the bed Carly slept in says 11:39. Nearly noon, fucking hell.

The bathroom door opens, steam curling out, and Carly emerges like something from a movie. She's wrapped in a towel, legs and shoulders bare, and my heart thumps. But she looks so different, her hair hacked into a punky short cut, bleached platinum.

"Oh, you're finally up." She pops one hip, looks left and right. "You like?"

I try to ignore the things her body is doing to me and concentrate on the new look. "Actually, it really suits you."

"Yeah, I think so too." She points to the table I took the chair from last night. The chair is back and there are paper sacks on the desk. "Bagels, pastries, some ham and cheese and shit."

"You went out before you changed your look?"

"I was starving, man. Don't worry, I borrowed your cap and hoodie. Eat, then I'll fix your hair."

I raise an eyebrow but choose not to argue. She's taking to all this pretty well. Maybe she's enjoying the freedom. Ironic that for her freedom is being on the run. The food is good and there's coffee, long since gone cold, but I gulp it down anyway. She goes back to the bathroom with more new clothes, comes out dressed in tight black jeans, a white T-shirt and short leather boots. She looks hot. The leather jacket she bought before is on the bed, along with a small sports bag with her other stuff. She's taking good care of herself, and I'm happy if she's using my cash for that. A paranoid part of me wonders if she isn't maybe getting ready to run, but if she is, there's really not much I can do about that. I have to trust her.

When I've eaten, she guides me to the bathroom and sits me on the edge of the bath. The scissors make short work of my hair, then she lathers and shaves my head. It feels weird, I've never been bald before.

"You look really different already." Her head is tipped to one side.

"Better?"

She snuffs a little, lips pressed together then, "Not really for me to say."

Something bites deep inside. Caitlyn used to do that, the little non-laugh through the nose. Carly and Caitlyn couldn't really be more different, but right then she let out a mannerism that felt like a knife in the guts.

Something stings my cheek and I'm looking into Carly's wide eyes under that new white hair. "Don't you fucking dare!" she yells, and I realize she slapped me.

"What?"

"I saw it in your eyes. Do not blank on me again, Eli. I can't take it any more."

She's right, I was going under. I need to avoid that more than anything else, and that means not thinking about the little stuff, the details, the minutiae. Caitlyn and Scottie are dead. That punch in the heart is all I can allow, all I can use to drive me towards Vernon Sykes.

Carly raises her hand to strike again, but I gently take her wrist. "It's okay. I'm okay."

"Really?"

"Yeah. Just getting used to things, you know? Got to find a new normal."

She stares with narrow eyes for moment, then nods once. "Shave your face. Then we should maybe go."

They're standing behind me as I shave, once Carly has left and shut the bathroom door. I try to ignore them in the mirror, but they keep ducking left and right, leering at me, mocking me.

"You think that's going to help?" Officer Graney asks. "There's facial recognition software now, you know. You'll get picked up easy."

"That right?" Dwight asks. "Goddamn, the po-lice sure are cheating on every aspect of fightin' crime."

"*You* such a fucking loser, they don't even need technology," Sly says and Dwight rounds on him.

"Oh yeah? They didn't bust me! I was cruisin' until this shithead showed up and fuckin' shot me."

Graney laughs. "You have a rap sheet longer than an elephant's erect dick, Ramsey, you redneck fuckwit."

Alvin barks a laugh and shoves Dwight away. Sly, on the other side of Alvin, sticks his chest out. "You want another go? Didn't I whip your ass once already?"

I stare in the mirror trying to zone it all out, concentrate on getting neat lines to this new goatee. It's not something I've ever done before. How much do I leave under my chin?

Michael is still and I realize he's staring hard at me. I can't help pausing as I catch his eye.

"You ready for this?" he asks.

"Ready for what?"

"Anything. Everything. Whatever comes next."

"Sounds like maybe you don't think I am."

The others have stilled, quietened to hear.

"You want me to fail?" I ask Michael.

"You fucking killed me, man. We were brothers."

"You fucked up. You crossed Vernon. You know it was kill you or both die."

Michael shakes his head sadly. "I would have died before I killed you."

I swallow, something about his tone betraying the truth of that. "Really?" I ask eventually.

"What kind of man are you, really?" Michael's eyes are hurt.

Something hardens in me, I know the truth of what *I* did. "You're the one who fucked up. Why should I let you get me killed?"

"You shot me in the fucking head."

"Yeah, and I lived to tell the tale. Now it comes all the way around and I plan to shoot Vernon Sykes in the head."

"You think that'll make things right?"

I look away from his hurt gaze. "It'll make things over."

Carly bangs on the door. "How long does it take?"

"I'm done." It's a pretty neat job as far as I can tell. It'll have to do anyway. Within minutes, we're in the car and gone.

I look like a badass with a bald head and goatee. I think it suits me, but it's not really the way I want to look. Though given the mop of curly hair I used to have, it makes a stark difference, and that's all that matters.

"Watch the road."

I pull my eyes from the rearview mirror and straighten up in the lane.

Carly's grin is a little crooked. "Can't stop looking at yourself."

"I've never looked like this before."

She pulls down the sun visor, checks herself in its mirror, then flicks it back up. "Yeah, it's a bit weird. Best to ignore it."

"You're probably right."

We drive in silence for a while as I find my way to the interstate.

"So where are we going?" Carly asks as I floor it up to the speed limit and sit in the right-hand lane.

"Charlotte. We need to head back south, but not all the way to New Orleans. Not yet. I know there's a Desert Ghosts clubhouse in Charlotte."

"That's a long way from Tweezer's club though, isn't it?"

"Yeah, but he's known there. I used to do weed runs for Vern and one of the buyers was the Desert Ghosts up in Charlotte. I would sell to Tweezer and he'd take it up there. He blabbed a lot about all the people he sold to."

Carly frowns. "You don't think that's too close to Vern, do you?"

"No, that's the beauty of it. None of the guys in Charlotte know jack about me or Vern. They only know Tweezer. I'm just a name as far as they're concerned, assuming Tweezer blabbed about me too. They've never seen me. But I know it's a place where we can ask after him. We'll have to wait and see what happens."

"Long drive."

"About six hours."

We lapse into silence, and I try to ignore the five assholes lined up in the over-sized cavern of the back seat.

"Shoot me in the fuckin' head then use my contacts, cocheese," Dwight says, and spits.

As if they're his contacts. His connection to the club, to Tweezer, is vague at best. I don't think he's ever even met them. Just because I'm talking about the weed he grew, he thinks he has some stake in it. Jesus, to think I was deeply entwined with people like this my whole life until now. Makes me sick. I turn on the radio, find a blues station and crank it. Carly looks at me sidelong, so I flick up one eyebrow at her. She chooses not to say anything.

We stop for drink, food, and piss breaks but don't say much all the way down. I think we're both happy to be moving forward instead of running in circles. It's difficult not to think too much, but I refuse to blank on her again and so I train myself to focus on other things. By the time we've hit Charlotte, I think I've fantasized just about every possible outcome of this meeting and everything that may follow, but I'm no more prepared for it than I was when I woke up this morning.

It's dark, nearly 9:00 p.m., when we cruise past the clubhouse and case the place.

"We can't just walk in there," Carly says. "Not like biker clubhouses are open bars."

"No, but they'll go out, I expect, head somewhere. We'll follow someone."

On our third pass, the chain-link fence is sliding open and three black and chrome Harleys thunder out and power up the street. I fall into place behind them, letting a few other cars separate us. It's a fairly easy tail.

"What if they're just going out for milk or something?"

I shake my head. "Carly, you need to learn patience. Play the odds. All this stuff, it's like a game. Or a sport. Think about fishing. You don't expect to haul a fish in every time you throw a line. It takes a few tries, maybe a few places. It takes patience."

She huffs, slumps down into her seat.

After a few minutes, one of the bikes peels off with a wave and the other two head on, making their way towards the outskirts of the city.

"Traffic's getting thinner," Carly says, and she's right.

I drop back a little further, start to guess at the occasional junction. But I've done this a lot, I'm pretty good at it. As I make a left in an industrial backwater, the two bikes are parked against the curb and the bikers stand on the footpath, one lighting a cigarette. Without pause I keep going.

"Don't look out the window," I tell Carly. "Count out loud one to ten."

"Seriously?"

"Just do it."

As she gets to four we're passing the bikers, both staring straight ahead. They glance up as we pass, I see them in the side mirror, but their eyes don't linger.

"Why did you have me counting?"

"So your mouth was moving as we passed like we were having a normal conversation. If I'd asked you to talk, make it look like a conversation, you'd probably have clammed up wondering what to say and we'd have looked suspicious."

She scowls at me and I shrug. I know I'm right. After a minute, she knows it too.

I make a right half a block down and pull up on the other side of the road in deep shadows between two streetlights. I can just see the bikes parked back there. Carly's smart enough not to ask what now. She knows we have to wait. My fishing analogy is holding up.

After half an hour, she says, "Starting to get old."

"Yeah. We'll give it a bit longer."

Another fifteen minutes and the two of them emerge again, laughing at some shared joke. The one has another cigarette while the other makes a phone call. He talks with his hands a lot, gesturing up and down, left and right, but it all seems good natured. He hangs up, slaps his buddy on the shoulder. That one drops his cigarette, grinds it under a scruffy black boot heel and they get on their bikes and head back the way they came.

It's not long before they're back in the clubhouse and we've learned nothing. I can feel Carly's frustration, but she's not talking. "Hungry?" I ask her.

"Yeah."

We go to a McDonald's, eat our fill, use the bathroom, and head back out. It's nearly eleven when the gates open again. We're parked up across one corner, masked by shadows. Another group of bikes roars out, five of them this time, and head into town. Ten minutes later and we're at the back of a parking lot, the bikes lined up at the front under the neon of a sign advertising JEM'S BAR. They're laughing and bumping fists with others already there.

"Hooked a fish on our second cast."

Carly glances at my smug grin and shakes her head. "Now what?"

"This is obviously a place they hang out, so we act like we just wanna hang out here too. You okay to play my girlfriend? It'll stop people sleazing onto you."

"Fucking sucks that I have to be your property to be left alone. Can't I just say I'm not interested?"

I stare at her till she subsides. "Hey, I agree, society is fucked. But right now we have other crusades."

"Fine, I'm your bitch."

"They aren't rappers, they're bikers. You're my old lady. Just hang on me, fawn a little, make it obvious, and it won't be thing."

She scowls. "I can do what's needed. What do we do inside?"

"I'll case it out a bit first, but I'll just find a good time to ask if any of those guys have seen Tweezer. Tell them I have a deal going with him, spin some shit. See what we learn."

It's loud inside, a rock band playing covers on a stage on the far side of the wide open space. There's hundreds of people, the lights low but not too low. The stink of beer, perfume and aftershave permeates the air. The music isn't quite enough to entirely cover the hum of conversation and the rattle of glasses, at least not up the back near the bar. The bikers are all gathered in a knot around two tables in one corner, about as far from the stage as they can get. A few of their old ladies are lounging around with them, some other young girls who look like maybe they'd like to become attached are flitting about like moths around flames. A lot of beer, hair, beards, tattoos, and laughter are on display. It's all about as amiable as I can imagine given the context.

Carly holds my hand, her fingers soft and warm, but her grip strong. She leans into me as we stand at the bar, runs her free hand over my shoulder possessively. She's good at this stuff. Part of me feels a thrill at her touch, the rest of me trembles inside, refusing to let memories of Caitlyn surface. Among it all is guilt. Caitlyn would rip the face off any girl she saw acting like this. But Caitlyn is dead, Carly can do what she likes, what does it even matter?

I grunt as pain whines into my thigh, a sharp knee from Carly. She's looking up at me with hard eyes. "Bar girl wants your money, honey." Her voice is singsong, but her gaze is ice. I was starting to blank again.

I hand over cash and we pick up our beers. "You gonna lose it here?" she asks me.

"No, I got it." I hope I sound more confident than I feel.

I lean back against the bar, make a show of enjoying the band a little. Halfway through my beer, I draw a long breath.

"Okay, let's do it."

Snaking my fingers to entwine with Carly's again, I pull her over to the tables in the corner. My stride is confident, but not arrogant, my face open but not weak. Several bearded Desert Ghosts look up at our approach, and the general conversation among them all dwindles.

"You got the wrong tables," one of them says, his beard down almost to his navel. He's that frightening combination of fat and muscle, maybe fifty years old but looks like he'd still win a wrestling match with a bear.

"Just wanted to ask a quick question."

"Wrong fucking tables, man." The tension ratchets up.

I notice the guy speaking has the Sergeant-At-Arms badge on his leather, putting him up there in the top of his chapter. Only the President and Vice-president of his club would rank higher. I hold his eye. "I don't want any drama, just a quick chat. I'm looking for a friend of mine. Friend of yours, too."

"That right?"

Carly's fingers tighten around mine, her eyes are a little wide, fear setting in.

Some young punk leans forward in his seat, drags a palm from Carly's shoulder to her elbow. "This one's pretty!"

He's drunk, stupid. As he twists to leer at his boss I can see his back patches. He hasn't earned all his colors yet. Desperate to please, a Prospect trying to boost himself up.

Without looking at him, I say, "Touch my woman again and you'll be shitting teeth for a week."

Sergeant-At-Arms barks a laugh, others around the two tables look amused or annoyed in equal measure. This is the test, this is the establishment of a temporary pecking order. Here's where they'll decide to talk to me, or destroy us.

"The fuck you say?" Young Punk demands. He stands up, all chicken chest and furious eyes.

Sergeant-At-Arms looks from me to him and back again.

Still not deigning to look at the fool, I say it again. "Touch her once more, you shit teeth. If you're so stupid you can't understand that, just try. Now about my friend."

Sergeant-At-Arms grins. Young Punk pulls Carly aside, tries to step between us. He's decided his boys will have his back, too stupid to realize he's the meat in this hierarchy sandwich, I almost feel sorry for him.

"I'll touch whoever—"

That's as far as he gets before my fist slams into his face.

He makes a strange surprised cough, staggers back. Not wanting to seem uncommitted, I finally turn to look at him. He's staring, blood pouring from split lips. He starts to look towards his Sergeant-At-Arms but I punch him again, lead two knuckles aimed right at his mouth. It'll cost me, but I'm a man who keeps promises.

I feel his teeth snap and crack, they bite into the flesh of my hand. I hope this fucker doesn't have hepatitis or anything. But his eyes roll, he collapses back into the lap of another, who grunts and pushes the hapless fucker to the floor. Young Punk is rolling and howling, both hands clapped over his mouth, blood pouring between his fingers.

I turn back to Sergeant-At-Arms. "You guys have a good dental plan?"

"I guess we'll take care of him."

The tension is still high, twanging in the air like a tripwire, everyone waiting to see which way Sergeant-At-Arms will play it. I hope I made the right choice. Carly's frozen like a statue.

"I did warn him," I say, amiably enough, even though my blood is rushing and my heart thumps in my throat. Carly presses back against me like I can hide her from sight.

Sergeant-At-Arms nods. "You did at that." There's a heavy pause, pregnant with every flavor of violence. Then he says, "Who you looking for?"

Stress drains from the area like rainwater down a drain. Several around return to their beers and conversation, no longer interested. Some relax but keep paying attention. No one even looks at Young Punk as he gasps, sobs, tries to pull himself back into his chair. I watch from the corner of one eye, but he's subdued now. As long as he doesn't follow us when we leave, we'll never have to worry about him again.

"I'm looking for a pal who's with your chapter down in New Orleans, goes by the name Tweezer."

Sergeant-At-Arms purses his lips. "Tweezer, eh?"

"Yeah. I assume his mother gave him another name, but I wouldn't know what it is. He and I have done business quite a bit over the years, but the last week or two I've been trying to reach him and getting no answer. That's not like him."

"And you just happened to come by here?"

I gesture vaguely back over one shoulder. "We're on the road back south, stopped in for a beer and a rest. When I saw your colors, I thought I'd ask. I know Tweezer came up to Charlotte pretty regularly. He talked about it."

Sergeant-At-Arms's face darkens. "Tweezer talked altogether too fucking much."

I make a point of looking surprised, concerned. "Oh, really? He never told me about any of y'all's business or anything. Just that he would regularly run to Charlotte, Atlanta, some other places."

Sergeant-At-Arms nods again, sniffs. "Yeah, well, he won't be running anywhere again."

"Is he inside?"

"Inside a pine fucking box, yeah."

My heart thumps once, so hard I think maybe he could see it through my jacket. That's potentially bad for us. "What happened?"

"Why do you care so fucking much, man?"

"Just that we were kinda friends, you know. Not close, but I've known him a long time."

"And what was your name again?"

"Gary. Gary Baker." No idea where that came from. "I used to run around some stuff that Dwight Ramsey grew, if you know what I mean."

Sergeant-At-Arms frowns. "You think name-dropping some bunch of fucking losers will help your case? I never heard of no Dwight Ramsey."

"I don't have any case. Just looking out for a friend, you tell me he's dead. That's a surprise, you know?"

Sergeant-At-Arms rubs a hand over his long beard, takes a slow, casual gulp of beer. "Our mutual friend Tweezer got himself entangled in something that put him in New Orleans jail. While he was in there, a white supremacist asshole by the name of Carl Hildebrand whacked him. Dispute about tobacco is what I heard. Who cares? He's gone. Now it's time you got gone, I'm running out of goodwill towards strangers who make my Prospects swallow their teeth."

"He was warned," I remind him.

"He was. And now you've been warned. Fuck off."

"Fair enough. I'm sorry for your loss."

There are barks and guffaws around the two tables, much shaking of heads.

"Find somewhere else to drink tonight," Sergeant-At-Arms says.

"Okay. Thanks." I pull on Carly's hand and haul her away. "Let's go, baby."

As we go, I whisper, "Glance back, look scared, but see if any of them get up to follow us. If I look back it'll seem weak."

Her hand is still trembling in mine, but she says, "Okay."

After a few more paces, as I put my glass on the bar and head for the door, she turns to look around. I yank her towards me for effect, eliciting a genuine, "Hey!"

Before she can berate me, I ask, "Anything?"

"Yeah. Looked like he was giving two of them the nod to follow us. They've got up and are strolling behind."

"They might jump us in the parking lot. Prepare for that. If I let go of your hand, you dive away from me instantly, understand? It means I'll need room."

"Okay. Jesus."

The night outside is cold, an icy bite to the breeze. The lot is well-lit, but not many people around. After the first couple rows of cars, heading for ours at the back, I turn around. The two Desert Ghosts are sitting astride their bikes, watching us. I tip my head, give them a "What?" expression. They don't even blink.

"Looks like they plan to follow us, not jump us here," I say to Carly. "Let's go."

As I start the car I hear the roar of the two Harleys firing up. As I leave the lot, they pull in behind, making no attempt to hide the fact.

"What do we do?" Carly asks.

I sigh. "I'm a little offended he only sent two."

She looks at me, but doesn't say anything.

The five idiots are lined up in that oversized back seat again when I next check the mirror.

"More deaths on your hands?" Officer Graney asks. Smoke curls from the hole in his throat as he hands a joint back along the row.

"I hope these guys fuck you up, cocheese," Dwight says. He draws deep on the joint, then holds one finger up. "In fact," he says, voice tight as he holds in the smoke, "I hope they fuck you, *then* fuck you up."

Alvin takes the joint. "You're a twisted freak," he says to Dwight.

"But do you disagree with me?"

"I don't want to watch anyone fucking anyone, but I would gladly watch this fucker die."

"Me too." Sly takes his hit, offers the joint to Michael.

Michael sighs, shakes his head. He looks at me with a questioning gaze.

"Yeah, I may have to kill them to save myself," I say.

Graney laughs, shakes his head. "You're racking up a real body count here."

"I get the feeling I've barely started."

Carly's brows are knitted. "What?"

I snap my attention back to her, back to the road ahead. "Nothing, just thinking out loud."

"Kill them?" she asks.

The back seat is empty, the two Harleys large in the rear window, staying close. I put my foot down a little, pushing to the top of the speed limit, and make a turn to lead us out of town.

"What if they're armed?"

I shrug. "I'm sure they are. Shouldn't matter."

"Was all this worth it? Did we learn anything? I mean, we know Tweezer is dead and that's maybe bad for us, but what else?"

"We know that Carl Hildebrand killed Tweezer. I know that name. Neo-Nazi fucker Vernon has used before to take out someone in New Orleans Parish Prison. It's one of the worst jails in the country, a real shit pit. Vern has some influence there. So we've learned that someone got word to Carl Hildebrand that Tweezer needed to die, and Carl Hildebrand fulfilled the request. Argument over tobacco, my ass. Whatever Carl got from Vern must have been worth it, but that evil fucker may well have done it for fun once the order came down. Regardless, if we can find whoever got word to Carl Hildebrand, we should be able to find Vern, right?"

Carly shakes her head, lips pursed. "But not Vern himself maybe. He would have used someone else."

"Sure, but we're getting closer. It's like unraveling a knot, you have to take it one thread at a time."

"And as Tweezer is dead, Vernon is free to build up his strength again. We probably don't have much time."

"We may already be facing a back-to-strength Vernon. But does that change anything?"

She shrugs.

Finally the town falls behind and the road ahead stretches long and dark, the last lights of Charlotte fading. No other traffic shares the tarmac except the two Harleys on my tail. Maybe this is where they'll make a move. I won't chance it. I press the accelerator harder, roaring away to make a run for it, see if they're just watching me out of town. The engine note of the Harleys goes up to match me, sticking close. No way I can outrun two powerful bikes like that. But that's okay.

"Put your hands on the dash, Carly?"

"What?" Confused, but she complies all the same.

I stand on the brake, tires howling as we slide on the asphalt, the nose of the car diving down. Then the crunching impact and shattering glass as the two bikes slam into the back of us. One goes under, disappears from the view. The other flips up, the rider punching back-first into the rear window, bowing it in. Before he can fall through, I stand on the accelerator again and the car lurches forward, bumps over something. The biker on the trunk rolls off to sprawl in the road, bikes and broken glass all over. The trunk of our car stands up like a crooked flag, the back window hanging in like a hammock.

"Fucking hell, Eli!"

"I don't have time to fuck around."

"They dead?"

"Don't know. Don't really care."

"What if they were just following to make sure we left town?"

I pin her with my eyes. "I don't care, Carly."

She watches me, licks her lips, draws breath to speak, then pauses.

I look back to the road ahead, the wreckage of the Desert Ghosts already lost in the darkness. All I want is to find my way to Vernon Sykes and woe betide any fucker who does anything to interfere with that. My wife and my son will be avenged.

"Don't go," Carly says quietly.

"What?"

"Don't go. Don't blank on me."

I suck a long, deep breath in, push images of Caitlyn and Scottie from my mind. A gathering darkness I hadn't noticed quivers and recedes from the edges of my vision.

"You still here?" She sounds like a little girl.

"Yeah, I'm here. You keep doing that. You think I'm going under, talk me out of it."

"I'll try."

"And so will I."

We drive in silence for a long time, even the five dead amigos are conspicuous by their absence.

Eventually, Carly says, "Still here?"

"Yeah."

"So what's the plan?"

"We have to change cars again. We'll get pulled over for sure, the way this one's banged up now."

She nods. "Let's take a look."

I pull over and we climb out. The damage is pretty extensive, the rear quarter panels are all folded in, the trunk concertinaed up into the shattered mess of the back window. All the taillights on both sides are destroyed with the exception of one bulb, glaring defiantly white in the night.

"If we steal another car, we'll be at risk again," Carly says. There's a low level of accusation in her tone.

"I know. This car was good, it was clean."

"Now it's not."

I sigh, rub my head. I'm beginning to tire of all this, frustration gaining ground on determination. It doesn't mean I'll give up going after Vernon, but it does mean I might fuck up. Like this, now, a good car wrecked. That's a fuck up. I can't let myself slip. But I did need to lose those bikers.

"We got money for another car?" Carly asks.

"Yeah, maybe. If we can find some piece of shit for a grand or something."

"We gonna drive through the night in the meantime?"

"No. Let's not. Come on."

It takes another half hour to see a sign for a motel and I park a half mile away from it, wipe down the car as well as I can for prints. It's a half-hearted effort, really. With the bag slung over my shoulder, Carly carrying hers the same, we walk to the motel, check in and crash out without another word passing between us.

I'm woken by the sound of the shower again, and I take one myself after Carly emerges, dressed and ready. There's a fire in her eyes, she looks at me sidelong, but I don't question it. After the way I took out those bikes, I guess she's wondering how far I'm willing to go, how many risks I'm willing to take. I'm willing to take them all. But hopefully she'll know, above everything else, that I plan to kill Vernon Sykes. And then she'll be free. But I have to stop fucking up.

When I come out of the bathroom she holds up a local paper, points to an ad. We pack up and go to a public phone, call the number. It's just what we need. An hour later and we're driving a beat-up old Dodge that we bought for the last of my cash, but we're back on the road again. Clean again. For now.

"We going to need more money?"

I shrug, shake my head. "I guess so, just to eat and sleep if nothing else. But it's okay, we're heading back south. I've got a few bolt holes and stashes around we can raid."

"You said you knew about this Carl Hildebrand guy? What do you know?"

"Part of a pack of white supremacist fuckwits in Baton Rouge, that's it. And I have a good stash in Baton Rouge. We go and get some money first, then we'll talk to Hildebrand's friends."

She thinks about this for a while, then, "Is it a risk? Will they know you?"

"No. I only know Hildebrand and his crew by name and reputation. We've never met. I'm not sure how we'll find them, but I guess we ask around."

"Ask around for a white supremacist group? In Baton Rouge?"

There's a *hyuck* from the back seat. "Y'all gonna get shot to death, cocheese," Dwight says, idiot face twisted in glee. If anyone knew about other racist shitbags, it would be him.

"I should kill you myself," Sly says.

Dwight flips him off. "Can't kill what's already dead."

"I can have fun trying."

"Don't start again, you two," Officer Graney says.

"You know where I can find 'em?" I ask Dwight.

"What?" Carly says.

Dwight howls laughter. "Oh, cocheese, you really want to go right to 'em? Yeah, I do know Carl Hildebrand. We've rallied together. His crew hangs out at a vehicle spray shop called Carl's Paints, somewhere on the outskirts of the city. Can't wait to see what happens there!" He sits back, rubbing his hands together.

Now he's mentioned it, it does ring a bell, somewhere back in my memory.

"Who are you talking to?" Carly asks. She looks at me, at the mirror, turns to look into the empty back seat.

"Just thinking out loud. I've remembered where I can look for Hildebrand's people. But we'll have to be careful what we ask and how."

My stash in Baton Rouge is a locker in the back of a comic store, owned by an old school pal. We stayed kind of close for a while, though I slowly dropped out of that circle. Most importantly, he's got nothing to do with the life, no connections to Vernon Sykes. I hope my stash is still there. His eyebrows raise as I enter the shop, he takes a moment to recognize me.

"Goddamn, I thought maybe I'd never see you again, man!"

He comes around the counter and we go from a tentative handshake to a brief hug. "Sorry it's been so long Jeff."

Jeff grins. "Life, right? I know how it is. You look different with a bald head! Suits you. I'm glad you're not dead."

"Me too. How are things?"

We make small talk for a while, I introduce Carly as my girlfriend, Clare. Jeff nods approval and she stays mostly quiet. After a few minutes I make a rueful face. "I'm sorry I can't stick around for long right now, but I'll come back soon and we'll catch up properly, yeah?"

"Sounds good, man."

"Meanwhile, you still got that stuff I left here?"

Jeff nods, bites his lower lip. "I was tempted to open it up after it had been so long. Over two years, now."

ALAN BAXTER

"Did you?"

"Open it? Nah. You know where it is."

I tell Carly to wait for me and go through to the back. The locker isn't locked, just standing half open beside a small fridge. My bag is in there, like an overnight bag for travelling, a padlock holding the zipper closed. I sling it over my shoulder and head back out.

"Thanks, Jeff."

"You really gonna come back and catch up properly?" he asks.

I pause before answering. We go back a long way, Jeff and me, we have history. He was a good pal, and he's right, I've ignored him for over two years. "I'm really gonna try," I say eventually.

He nods. "You okay, dude?"

"Right now? Not really. But I hope to be soon."

"Always cold beers in the fridge."

I clap his shoulder. "Thanks, man. I'm looking forward to those." I mean it, but he can see the doubt in my eyes.

Back in the car, I check the bag before we pull away. No idea where the key might be, so I use my pocket knife to slice it open alongside the zipper. A couple of changes of clothes, a pair of sneakers, toothbrush and other toiletries, a snub-nosed .38 and five grand in cash.

Carly whistles low. "Handy."

"Yeah. I've got a few of these around the area, but only this one had a decent amount of money in it. It'll see us right for now." I pocket the cash, leave everything else in the bag and drop it behind the passenger seat. "Let's go. I'm hungry."

"Lunch first, then white supremacists?"

"Sounds like fun."

After lunch I look up Carl's Paints and we drive over there. Plenty of people around in various businesses, junkyards and delivery warehouses, all with wide concrete aprons out front. Trucks and cars move in and out between chain-link fences. Carl's is at the end of a row, a big sign with the name in airbrushed chrome and red fire. A few cars sit out front waiting, a Harley with a skull and mist design on the tank right by the door. A young skinhead with a white-collared shirt and jeans sits in a chair leaned back against the wall of the office. The shirt sleeves are rolled down and closed at the wrists, no doubt concealing swastika tattoos from the general public. He's taking in the sun, though the day is cool, and smoking a cigarette. No one else seems to be around.

"A white supremacist getting a tan," Carly says. "The irony."

I park the car and the kid tips his chair forward, looks disdainfully at the crappy Dodge we're driving.

"How do we do this?" Carly asks.

I grin at her. "Reckon my new haircut might help me out?"

She huffs that humorless laugh. "Good luck with that."

"Play it by ear, see how it goes."

The roll-up front of the paint shop is closed, no one else visible in the office. As we get out of the car, I see the five ghosts lined up along the chain-link, like an audience at a show. Michael and Officer Graney look bored, their bloody wounds glistening in the sun. Sly is staring at the paint shop kid with undisguised hatred.

"You kill this fucker for me," he says. "Consider it a payback."

"I don't owe you anything," I mutter as I pass.

Carly frowns at me, but says nothing.

Alvin Crake and Dwight Ramsey are the two most interested, Dwight almost slavering like a dog.

"You gonna fuck this up and get killed right here, cocheese!" he says.

I ignore him.

"Help ya?" The kid has a strangely high voice, like it never really broke, though he must be at least seventeen or eighteen.

"Maybe. Who's in charge here?"

"Me."

"No, seriously."

He bristles and Dwight *hyucks*. If he wasn't already dead I'd kill him again right now. My gun is tucked in the back of my jeans, under my jacket, but it'll stay there unless this kid causes trouble. I swallow, realize I'm angry and ready to kill. I need to not fuck up.

"I think that piece of shit needs more than a paint job," the kid says, jutting his chin at my car.

"I'm not here for paint."

"What you want then?"

"You really here alone right now?"

The kid sneers. "Yeah, I'm holding the shop. The others are… out."

"When are they back?"

He stands up, decides to act hard. "What do you care?"

Big mistake. My hand clamps around this throat and I slam him back against the white brick wall. He grunts and fear widens his eyes. Carly turns to watch the driveway and the road, ready to warn me if anyone comes, I figure. Good girl.

"Fuckin' hell," Dwight says, the wind gone from his sails. "Couldn't be timed worse!"

I grin. Couldn't be timed better in my opinion.

"What are you smiling at, man?" the kid asks. I can see the top of an Iron Cross tattoo on his neck where I'm stretching it out of his collar.

"I'll ask the questions, you answer."

"Fuck you!"

My free hand finds my gun and I jam the barrel up under his chin. His jeans stain instantly with piss. "You will answer me."

"Okay, man, okay. What do you need?"

"What's your name?"

"Kevin!"

"Okay, Kevin. A friend of mine, you don't need to know who, has to get some information to Carl Hildebrand." Kevin's eyes betray his recognition. "Yeah, you know Carl. So do I. See how we're all friends here? So stop acting like a prick. Now here's the thing. I need to get word to Carl about something too, so who among you lot would I see about that? Unofficial word, obviously, so don't suggest I just go up to New Orleans Parish like a common visitor."

Kevin swallows hard against my palm, I feel his Adam's apple bob desperately. "I don't know, man. I only know Carl's name by conversation." I squeeze harder, he yelps. "But Gene will know."

"Gene?"

"Yeah, yeah. Gene. He'll help you get word to Carl, for sure. I know he's done that stuff before."

"And where is Gene?"

Kevin starts to grin just as Carly says, "Hey, Eli. Trouble."

I turn to see a white van pull into the small lot. Three dudes with bald heads and lots of tattoos are lined up all along the front seat, faces twisted in hate at the sight of me holding young Kevin by the neck. Dwight starts dancing from foot to foot, laughing and saying how this is more like it.

I drop Kevin and slip the gun back into my jeans, hopefully before they feel the need to pull theirs. This was going so well. The three pile out and two more leap from a sliding door at the side. They line up across the concrete looking at me and

Kevin runs to join them. Six of them in a line, the paint shop at our backs, the road out front empty. This has turned very bad indeed.

"The fuck is happening here?" the one in the middle demands. He glances at Kevin's wet jeans, sneers.

Kevin leans forward. "Gene, this guy threatened to kill me, says he knows Carl Hildebrand."

Gene doesn't take his eyes from me this time. "Shut up, Kevin." At least now I know which one is Gene. He's the only one I need to talk to.

Gene's fingers flex at his side. I know a draw tell when I see one, the guy is itching to grab the gun in his waistband. The others are looking from him to me and back again, waiting for orders.

"Why don't we all go inside?" Gene says.

I don't like that idea at all, out of sight and heavily outnumbered. "I just need to know how—"

"I don't give a fuck what you need! Turn around and walk in that office door now."

The door next to where Kevin was sitting when we arrived is ajar. There's a desk and filing cabinets in there, another door, wide open, leading directly to the paint shop, which only has one car in it, though room for three or four. A closed off spray room fills one back quarter.

"Eli," Carly says, her voice thin.

"Come on." I turn and walk in, taking her hand as I go. "First chance you get, you run. The keys are in the ignition. Understand?"

"Eli..."

"Understand?"

"Yes."

"Go through," Gene says and we enter the big space and turn to face them.

"We got off to a bad start, Kevin and I. Let's maybe try again."

"One kid and you've got an attitude and a gun, now you want to play nice?"

I raise my hands, palms up. "The kid has a mouth, pissed me off."

They all laugh at that and Gene nods. "He's a pain in the ass, but little brothers, eh? What can you do?" He holds out a hand. "Now how about you give me that gun?"

There's no way I can let that happen, and I know there's going to be blood. I can see it in Gene's eyes, he doesn't give a fuck about us. He plans to hurt us, probably rape Carly, there's no negotiating here. I know bad people when I see them. I fucked up again. Truth is, now I can either fuck up completely, or get lucky.

I reach slowly behind my back, watching the twitch of the others here. "Carly, run."

I pull the gun quickly and dive to one side. Surprise is my only advantage. Dwight whoops, Alvin laughs like a hyena. Sly coughs on his joint smoke.

I'm firing as I roll to the cement, two of the fuckers dead with holes between their eyes, but then the others are drawing. Gene is fast and furious, Kevin drops and cowers, unarmed and terrified. The two remaining neo-Nazi fuckers both leap in opposite directions, both pulling hand cannons. Death or glory now.

I try to draw a bead on one, but my peripheral vision picks up their movement and I can't fire, have to keep rolling. Cement chips spit up from where I just was. Carly is running, but not for the door. She's leaping for the cover of the one car in here. Fuck it! If nothing else, she was supposed to get away, to survive.

Gene is yelling something I can't make out over the booming gunshots, then fire sears along my right calf. I fire twice, miss once, but kneecap one of the fuckers with my second shot. He screams like a schoolgirl on a rollercoaster, the sounds is staggeringly surreal.

But Gene and the other one have got me in their sights, I'm out of time, out of options. The ultimate fuck up. For fuck's sake, Carly, run. But then she pops up from behind the car and one neo-Nazi looks suddenly stunned with a bullet hole right over his heart. A rivulet of scarlet runs down his shirt and he collapses. Carly has the .38 from the bag I picked up at Jeff's and she's a damn fine shot.

My gun tracks to Gene, and so does hers. Suddenly he's outgunned, teeth bared as he was about to murder me. Now he pauses. The kneecapped one is squirming on the cement, howling like a whipped dog, blood spreading in a fast-growing pool. Kevin is still huddled against one wall, hands clasped over the back of his head, shivering violently. The rest, bar Gene, are dead. Goddamn. Way to go, Carly.

There's a tense pause but for Kneecap's howling, then he slowly winds down. He tries to sit up, sees the mess his leg has become, and passes out. The silence is sudden and physical. Gene, Carly and me, we're locked in a Mexican standoff. He's outgunned two to one, I can tell he's trying to decide whether he should pull the trigger or not. I'm dead if he does, no way he'll miss. I'll fire too and hopefully I won't miss. But Carly will also fire, and judging by her last shot, she definitely won't.

I draw a shaky breath, my calf throbbing with pain. I daren't look at it yet. "If you shoot me, you die. She'll get you. Lower your gun and we'll talk."

He growls, low in his throat like a cornered dog. Then hisses and drops his gun to clatter onto the cement. "This is fucking insane!"

From the corner of my eye, I can see that Carly is starting to shake. Shock and adrenaline rushing through. I wonder if she's ever shot someone before. I'm going to have to find out where she learned to shoot, but targets and humans elicit a very different response. I need to give her something to do.

I keep my gun on Gene. "Carly, go staunch his blood loss. And get Kevin over there in the corner, keep an eye on him."

She nods, Kevin puts himself in the corner, eyes wild, while Carly grabs some rags from a bench and ties up the poor bastard's knee. He's weak and slurry, moaning and crying. I stand up, ignoring my own hurt, glance around. "Three of your boys are down and done," I say. "That one will never walk the same again, but he'll live if you're quick."

Gene is literally shaking with rage, his face is red like he's sunburned. He'll have a heart attack or aneurysm the way he's going. "The fuck *are* you?"

"Your worst nightmare. You shouldn't have acted so tough and brought us in here." I gesture at the dead and injured. "This is all your fault, I got nothing to lose. So tell me what I need to know and you can maybe save that one."

He growls again. "What if I don't care about him?"

I swing my arm around to level my gun at Kevin. "Little brothers, eh? What are you gonna do?"

His eyes widen. "You fuck!"

"Talk or he dies."

"What do you want?"

I already know how all this will go down, I don't have time

for niceties. "I know you got word to Carl Hildebrand in the Parish to kill Tweezer, the Desert Ghost."

His anger turns to confusion. "That's what this is? You a biker? The fuck that have to do with you?"

"Who told you to tell Carl to kill Tweezer?"

He tips his chin up. "You really avenging some piece of shit, two-bit, fucking loser biker?"

"No. I don't care about him."

Realization dawns. "Oh, you're after whoever wanted Tweezer dead. I honestly can't help you. I don't know who sent the order down."

"Sure, you maybe don't know who it was, but someone passed on that message. Someone came to you and said Tweezer needs to die, and they told you to tell Hildebrand to do it. They're the next link in the chain. Who is that?"

"I tell you that, I'm dead."

I gesture with my gun at Kevin. "You don't tell me, he's dead."

He stares at me and he sees where this is going. Sees the only place it can go. A strange calm descends over him. "You'll let Kevin go?"

"Tell me what I need and he lives. But I'll be taking him with me, so if your information turns out to be bullshit, he dies after all."

I watch the last of his defiance drain out. He looks past me. "Kevin. Kevin!" The kid looks up, face the color of ash. Gene smiles. "You do whatever this guy says, okay? And then you'll be okay."

"Gene?" Kevin's voice sounds more like he's seven than seventeen.

Carly looks up from where she's trying to stop the blood flowing out of that ruined knee. Her mouth falls open and she steps away, makes like she's going to say something then shakes her head and moves to a sink to wash the blood off her hands.

"You hear me, Kevin?" Gene says. "Do exactly what he says."

"Okay, Gene."

He looks back to me. "You promise me. He's too young to know better. You let him live."

"If what you tell me is true."

He nods, swallows. "Kevin, you take this guy to see Simon Clarke."

"The retard?"

"Don't call him that. But yeah. You can do that?"

"Sure, I can do that. You'll be okay?"

"Yeah, little brother. I'll be okay. You just take this guy to Simon."

"Okay."

Kevin stands, his legs flapping together like flags in a storm.

I catch Carly's eye. "Take Kevin out to the car, start it running. Keep your gun on him."

She stares at me hard for a beat, then drops her gaze. She hooks the little .38 at Kevin. "Come on."

When they've gone, Gene looks at me with undisguised venom. "Fuck you, you piece of shit."

I know he's told me the truth. As the car outside roars into life, I jam my gun barrel into his chest to muffle it as much as possible and shoot his heart out. He drops with hate still burning in his eyes. The kneecapped guy on the floor has passed out again. I crouch and hold his nose and mouth closed for a count of one hundred, watch the pulse in his neck slow down and stop. Officer Graney was goddamned right about a rising body count, but these guys would be too good at getting word out ahead of me. Besides, they started this. I collect up their guns before

I leave, five variations on nine-millimeter semi-autos, all with full clips of ammo. The bullet wound in my calf is thankfully superficial, despite the roaring pain of it. I strap it up with a clean rag and leave.

Carly is in the front passenger seat of the Dodge, twisted around to keep her gun on Kevin. Exhaust curls up from the tailpipe. I drop into the driver's seat and say, "So, where do we find Simon?"

"Gene's okay?" Kevin asks.

"He'll be right in there waiting for you to get back. Now which way?"

"Head out to the main road and hang a right."

All his attitude and bravado are gone, but I'm more worried about Carly. How long can she hold it together before what she did in there catches up with her? I glance over and she catches my eye, nods once, teeth pressed hard together. Muscles twitch in her cheeks. Damn, she's strong. She's not happy, far fucking from it, but she's strong. I head for the main road.

"Where'd you learn to shoot like that?"

She grimaces. "Vern used to let me shoot targets out back all the time. I enjoyed the sense of power, played with all kinds of guns. He said it never hurt for a girl to know how to defend herself. Always a little nervous too, like maybe he was teaching me something I might use against him one day. But he knew it was important to keep me from getting bored, and I wanted to know how to shoot."

"You're good."

"I didn't know for sure until just then." She gulps, half laugh, half sob.

There's a heavy silence in the car for a while as we drive, except for the occasional direction from Kevin. His voice is small, all that audacity from outside the paint shop shattered like thin ice under a boot heel.

"How old are you, Kevin?" I ask eventually.

"Nearly sixteen."

Fucking hell. He really is a kid.

"Okay, Kev, now here's how it's going to go. Things got really messy back there, didn't they?"

"Are they really dead? Dylan and Sam and—"

"Don't think about that now, okay? There's business to take care of. I need your help, then you can go back and see about all that."

"They were going to hurt us, weren't they?" Carly says. "Be honest, Kevin."

In the mirror I watch tears well up in his eyes. Eventually he nods. "They've done it before."

Carly slumps a little, some measure of relief, I guess.

"Kevin!" His eyes snap to mine in the mirror. "Tell me about Simon Clarke."

"He's a retar... He's a mentally disabled guy that Gene knows. Used to be Carl Hildebrand would get work via Simon, now Gene does, since Carl got locked up. There's a few people, a few networks, you know? I don't know how it all breaks down, but there are a few trusted connections who act as intermim... inteminn..."

"Intermediaries."

"Yeah, that. Right. So one of those is Simon. He shows up now and then with instructions for Gene. Once Gene does whatever it is he's been asked to do, he lets Simon know, then Simon shows up with some money."

"And that way Gene never knows who actually contracted him for the work."

"Exactly."

"Bit of a risk, isn't it? Using someone mentally disabled for a job like that?"

"No, Simon's not an idiot or anything. I shouldn't call him a retard, Gene doesn't like it when I do. Simon's got the autistic, only he has it pretty bad. Can't touch people, never looks you in the eye, has to count fucking everything and shit like that. But he absolutely will get things done."

"But what if Gene got fingered by the cops and he turned Simon in? He wouldn't hold up much under interrogation would he?"

"I guess it depends how much he knows, right? How much he'd have to tell. He might not know who it is that gives him the information."

"Layers like a rotten fucking onion," Carly mutters.

I can only nod. "One step at a time," I tell her. I catch Kevin's eye again, then turn my attention back to the road as I say, "So here's how it goes. When we get to Simon, you're going to take him a message. You tell him it's from Gene."

"Is it? Turn left here."

"Yeah, it is. Me and Gene talked about it while you waited in the car. Simon does everything face to face, right? No discussions on the phone?"

"That's what he does with Gene. Just calls and asks to catch up. I don't know where."

"Okay. So you tell Simon that Gene talked with Carl Hildebrand. Carl knows some stuff about Tweezer and thinks it's worth something. Tell him Gene wants to meet, and it's really urgent."

"Who's Tweezer?"

"You don't need to know the details. You tell Simon to meet

his contact and say that, then you come back and tell me what's what. You understand?"

"Yeah, I got it. Go left up ahead."

We turn into a fairly quiet-looking suburban street on the south side of Baton Rouge.

"We going to Simon's house?"

"His mom's house. Simon lives with her."

"He your age?"

"Nah, in his twenties or something."

"You fucking dumb, man?" Michael's voice is strange, it's the first time he's spoken to me in ages. I'm seeing double, Kevin in the real back seat, but that wide open space with the ghosts in it overlaid, coexisting.

I blink and look away. "What?"

Carly frowns at me, but I ignore her.

"In his twenties," Kevin repeats.

"Simon Clarke, man," Michael says. "Pauly Brand's nephew?"

A flood of realization hits me, but I don't say anything.

"You remember Pauly Brand," Michael says. "You opened his neck with a knife when everything went bad. Fiona Clarke is Pauly Brand's sister, she has an autistic son. That's too much of a coincidence to be random. Vernon is using Pauly's nephew as a runner."

"We're only one step away," I say, and the ghosts flutter and disintegrate, their mouths twisting, angry faces fading, annoyed they didn't get a chance to harangue me this time.

Carly is still frowning. "Are we?"

"I'll explain later."

"Here," Kevin says, pointing at a big house on a nice lawn.

"You remember what I said?"

"Yeah."

"Then go, and come right back."

After a minute, Kevin is standing at the door talking to a young man with a dark bowl cut and Pokemon T-shirt. It must be Simon, he's starring at his shoes, nodding short, sharp nods, hands clenching and unclenching at his thighs.

"This gonna work?" Carly asks.

"Hopefully. Simon sets up the meet, we follow whoever turns up when they leave."

"And after this," she gestures at the front step, "we don't need Kevin any more." Her eyes are challenging.

I look away, see Simon go back inside, close the door without looking up. Kevin comes back to the car.

"Simon says he'll call his contact and pass it on. But he says the contact will not be happy about Gene wanting to meet."

"What did you say?"

"Told him that's all I knew and they'd have to work it out."

"Good. You did well."

Kevin licks his lips, gaze darting between me and Carly. He's not stupid. "So can I go now? Will you take me back to Gene?"

"Not just yet."

I drive away, go around the block and pull up on an opposite corner to watch Simon's house obliquely from afar.

"We could be here a while," I say. "If you're quiet and well-behaved, Kevin, I'll let you go soon, okay?"

"Okay."

We sit without talking, staring at the house. I ignore the harassment of the ghosts in the back seat, refuse to even look in the mirror. I can't figure out why it's these five fools who plague me, I've killed many more men than them. Then a thought occurs to me: perhaps it's guilt. Of all the men I've killed, these five weren't trying to kill me. Weren't even planning to kill me.

They may be far from innocent, but did I take their lives unjustly perhaps, by some strange metric? Is that it? I cast a glance in the mirror and they're still and calm. Michael raises one eyebrow, as to say, *You think?* Graney toasts me with a bottle, Sly with his joint. Alvin and Dwight sneer. What does it really matter?

Thinking I'm staring at him, Kevin slumps against the door and closes his eyes. Carly alternately stares at the house and then her hands. Stillness envelopes us for a time.

"I've never done that before," she mutters after a while.

"I know." She's talking about killing someone. It never affects two people the same way. It had to come up in conversation sooner or later. "You wanna talk about it?"

She nods towards the back seat. "Not now."

"If it's any consolation, you're doing really well."

"Feel like I might crack into pieces."

"There'll be time for that later. You can wait?"

"Guess I'll have to."

I give her a soft smile. "It's okay to fall apart a bit. Normal." I remember vomiting into that potted palm. "But if you can hold it together for a while, that's good."

She takes a long shuddering breath and stares at her hands again.

It's over an hour before the front door opens and Simon steps out.

He's wearing a tweed jacket over his Pokemon shirt and shiny leather shoes below straight jeans. He's skinny and nervous, taking short, rapid steps off up the sidewalk. When he turns the corner, I cruise up to watch him standing at a bus stop. After a few minutes, he boards a bus and I follow. A sense of finality begins to descend, like we're heading into an endgame.

It's only a ten-minute bus ride for Simon, then he gets off

and goes into a doughnut shop. I pull up on the opposite curb, wondering where the best place to see will be. I catch my breath when a car door opens in the doughnut shop parking lot and big, black Charles gets out. Vernon Sykes's right hand man.

Carly gasps and I nod.

"Now we just have to follow him when he leaves." I quickly maneuver the car into a side street from where we can watch Charles's car.

"Once he comes back out, can I go?" Kevin asks.

"We'll see."

Carly flicks me a glance, face pained. Kevin just nods, frightened but smart enough to stay silent.

We wait.

It's not too long before Charles and Simon emerge together. Charles has a face like thunder, rage and frustration clear in his eyes, the set of his mouth. Simon seems just like he was outside his house. They exchange another couple of words and then Simon walks off across the parking lot, towards a bus stop to go back home.

Charles stands by his car, hands on top of his head, fingers laced together. He stares off into nowhere and I have a tight pulse of panic, think he's going to look right at us. But even if he sees this car, surely he can't recognize the occupants from this distance. He gives a quick shake of the head and gets in, slams the door.

"Can I go?" Kevin asks, a waver in his voice.

"Not yet." I start the engine, watch Charles pull out and turn south. I join the traffic flow to follow him, several cars behind. This is going to sorely test my tailing skills, I know how good Charles is at spotting a tail, because he taught me how he spots them. He taught me a lot, but maybe I can use that against him and do things differently. With any luck, he's not expecting to be followed.

"You're in deep shit now, cocheese." Dwight's drawl is worse than ever, his cheek distended with tobacco, a quart of Jack Daniels in one grimy fist. Where do ghosts get liquor? Where do they get joints?

"He's right," Alvin says, swigging from his own bottle. "You're gonna walk right into a hornet's nest and get stung all to fuck."

I ignore them, but maybe they're right. I have no way of knowing how well-protected Vernon is now, how much of a force he's gathered.

"You know how the man works," Sly says, eschewing bourbon for his ubiquitous spliff. Blue smoke clouds around his head, snagging tendrils in his afro. "He has connections, man. Even if he not operating at full strength again, he'll have a contingent of fucking soldiers. They'll be ready and willing to smoke you!" He gestures with the joint, takes a long draw and blows a cloud over me.

It's thick and pungent, makes me cough. I wave a hand to waft it away.

Carly frowns. "You okay?"

"You can't see that?"

"See what?"

I watch her for a second then look back at the road. "Nothing."

"What's happening, Eli?"

"There'll be a gunfight at the end of this."

"Yeah, I figured as much."

"You should wait it out, don't get involved."

"Fuck you, Eli."

I sigh.

"Dragging more people to early graves, eh?" Officer Graney

says. He takes a swig from Dwight's bourbon, grimaces, hands it back. "That body count going up and up. How long before it's you? Or her?"

I shake my head, refusing to answer.

"He's right, dude." Michael's face is pained. "So many deaths."

Better if we're all dead and gone, I think. Not like the world will miss us.

We join Interstate 10 heading south east and I realize where we might be going. About halfway between Baton Rouge and New Orleans is Lake Maurepas and the Maurepas Swamp Wildlife area. I10 runs right between the lake and the Mississippi River, through a small town call Laplace. North of Laplace, in the middle of nowhere, Vernon Sykes has a house with about ten acres of land around it. Old colonial place, hardly anyone knows about it except a few of his closest associates. He's not aware that I know about it, but I do, through a little gossip, a little adding two and two together and coming up with Laplace.

"I can't imagine we're going back to New Orleans, are we?" Carly says. "I mean, if Vern is back in town, that would mean he feels back up to strength."

I shake my head. "The place near the lake."

She looks over at me. "How do you know about that?"

I shrug. "Just do. I bet he's holed up there."

"With a fuckin' army!" Dwight says, then spits and cackles.

"I'd really like to get out," Kevin says. He looks pale, sick. "Just here on the highway, no problem. I'll hitch back."

"Sorry, Kev. You have to stay here just a while longer yet." I can't risk him maybe calling the wrong person, dropping us in it.

"What can you tell me about the place?" I ask Carly.

She purses her lips for moment, then, "It's a big old house, like something out of *Gone with the Wind*. White balconies and columns and shit. It's got a fence all 'round, high gate at the front that's controlled from inside the house. Long driveway, kinda twists its way up to the house, nice gardens close by, then nothing else except a bunch of cypress trees and grass."

"Any outbuildings?"

"Got a big-ass barn on one side, a three-car garage on the other, both detached from the house, but nearby. That's all. The gardens around the house itself are managed, all flowerbeds, a fountain, bushes and shit. There's a gardener's shed about two hundred yards from the back of the house."

"What's the fence like?"

"About six feet high, wooden palings."

"Easy to scale?"

"Sure. But the house has security lights all around, motion sensors, cameras, you know? It's not Fort Knox, you can get in easily, but you won't get close without being seen."

I think about that for a while. I guess maybe being seen is the least of my concerns. I just need to get in. And hope the odds against me aren't too ridiculous. I have a righteous need for vengeance and surely that will get me a long way on its own. Stupidity might get me the rest of the way. Or get me dead. Either way, I'm on a collision course I can't change now.

Sure enough, Charles heads north off I10 just before Laplace.

"You know how to get to the house from here?"

Carly nods. "Yeah, I've been there plenty. I remember the way."

I pull up and let Charles drive away. No point in risking him seeing us now we don't need to tail him. If he isn't going to that house, we might be in the shit again, but I feel pretty confident we're on the right track.

"We can't wait long," Carly says. "Once Charles reports back,

Vernon will get angry about Gene and start proceedings. Won't take him long to find out what's happened."

She's right. I'd like to wait for night, but that's not an option. I'll be doing this in broad daylight. "We'll give Charles ten minutes to get ahead of us and get inside."

Carly nods, but says nothing. Kevin is equally quiet, the ghosts absent.

Restless, ignoring the throb of the bullet burn across my calf, I give it eight minutes then pull away. Carly directs me and it's not long before she says, "About another mile up there, you'll see the gates on the left."

I don't slow down, cruise right by. She points as we pass, high white metal gates set in a couple of brick columns. Wooden fence like she described stretching away to either side. Numerous trees overhang the fence, fill the garden. Twisted branches of bald cypress trees, long beards of Spanish moss. The grass is a deep emerald green. It all looks so calm and peaceful, but it will run red before this day is done.

And I have to protect Carly from all of this. If nothing else, she needs to remain safe.

There's a small road a few hundred yards past the house and I pull in, park up in the shadow of some trees off the asphalt.

"So what's the plan?" Carly asks.

I stare straight ahead, knuckles white on the wheel.

"Eli? Eli, what are..? Oh no, come on, Eli! Not now!"

Without looking at her, I get out and pull open the back door. Kevin looks up at my face, sees something he really doesn't like and tries to scramble back, but I'm too fast. I grab his arm and haul him out. The ghosts are lined up by the trees, faces alive with glee.

"Oh yeah, let's have some fuckin' mayhem!" Alvin says.

Officer Graney and Michael are off to one side, both looking on with hooded eyes.

"What's happening," Kevin says, voice high and panicked. Piss stains the front of his jeans again, spreading like a blossoming flower. Poor kid. But this is for the best.

I hit him, not too hard, but right across the point of the chin, and he crumples like tissue paper, silent.

Carly is out of the car, screaming at me, not daring to come near.

I crouch, pull cable ties from my pocket. I've always got a whole bunch of them, tools of the trade. I secure Kevin's hands behind his back, then fix his ankles together. He seems to weigh nothing as I pick him up and dump him into the spacious trunk. Thankfully there's room for two in there.

Carly scrabbles in her pocket as I walk around the car for her, not looking at her, but past her. "No, Eli! No!" She manages to pull the .38 from her pocket, but I cuff her hand aside and the small gun flies off into the underbrush. It passes right through Sly and he laughs, deep and booming.

"Eli, no!"

It's hard, so hard, to show no emotion as I raise my other hand, this state of mind so hard to fake. But it's for the best. I want to apologize to her first, tell her this is for her own good, but it's all pointless. No time, and I can't trust myself to say anything right. Her eyes go wide and she opens her mouth to say something else, but I can't let her. Suppressing a grimace, I knock her out and tie her up too. Once she's in the trunk next to Kevin, I close it up, then unlatch the back of the rear seat. She won't find it right away, but if she thrashes around enough, she'll knock it open and find her way out. I haven't tied her feet, so maybe she'll be able to go for help. Hopefully I can come back and set them both free myself, apologize, put myself at their mercy. But right now, I have one focus.

I collect the five nine-millimeters I took off Gene and his crew, stuff two into my waistband, one into the top of each boot, carry the fifth. It takes only a minute to push through the trees and scrub and find my way to the side fence of Vern's house. Another minute and I've found the gardener's shed Carly told me about.

There's a fair amount of cover between the fence and that shed, maybe I can use the trees and shrubbery to get close. Maybe not. Who cares? Here goes.

I'm over the fence and into some dense shrubbery in no time at all. Carly said there were motion sensors, who knows what else, so I can expect company any time. I just need to make sure Vernon digs in and doesn't make a run for it under cover of their fire.

A quick sprint, crouched low, takes me past a bed of rose bushes and into the shadow of the gardener's shed. As I peek around the side of it, the back door of the house slams back and three guys come bursting out. I don't recognize any of them. I was hoping to get a bit closer than this. Perhaps I've made the worst fuck-up of all. But there was no time to plan, no opportunity for subtlety and stealth. Oh well.

Game on.

The three fan out from the door, pistols gripped double-handed, raised to eye level like FBI recruits on a practical exam. The one in the middle yells, "It's broad daylight, there's nowhere to hide!" and I put a bullet between his eyes. His face is more surprised than anything else as he falls, but I'm already rolling to the rose garden, firing again.

I'm a damn good shot, but rolling and shooting is a low-success maneuver. Even still, one of the other guys screams and spins to one side, his left arm a flood of blood.

"Keep moving!" the other one shouts.

I take his advice, roll again. Coming up onto one knee, I pause long enough to shoot him, then I'm up and running. His jaw disintegrates, and he howls and mewls as he stumbles and falls to his knees, hands trying to hold back a crimson waterfall, his gun dropped, forgotten. Shit, that was an ugly shot. The one with the arm wound is tracking me and he starts squeezing off shots. I hear them tear through the air by my face, but he's not quite good enough. A concrete fountain offers me cover and I take it. I count a beat of three then pop up and rapid-fire three holes into his heart.

I'm distracted by the one with his face shot off, sobbing and staring in disbelief at his red palms. Thankfully my peripheral vision catches a glint of light and I'm moving before I realize what it is. Then I'm scanning for it, see an upstairs window swinging open, two silhouettes moving inside. I empty the clip of the gun, destroying glass and frame alike before they can aim and fire.

The next gun comes free of my waistband as I run to the cover of the house and quickly put Jawless out of his misery. There's hate and relief in his eyes. That's a look that'll haunt me if I survive this.

Someone appears at the back door and would have got the drop on me but there's a crash to the other side. A steel wheelbarrow rocks on its side, Michael standing there beside it. Did he just kick that over? Regardless, the man emerging from the house spins toward it, unaware of me, and I shoot him point-blank.

Now I get to go inside. More cover, but more chance of ambush too. I pause for one long, deep breath, then duck in, my gun held before me, playing left and right across a big kitchen.

Brass and copper pans hang from the ceiling, an old black iron stove dominates one corner. Otherwise it's all modern, brushed aluminum and bright white. As white as the weatherboards cladding the outside and the balustrades of the balconies.

I pause, listen. Everything is eerily still. Surely that wasn't all of them? Only four. And no Charles yet. He'll be close to Vernon, that's his job. He's not a smart man, but he's strong as a bear and loyal as a dog. Vernon never keeps the really smart guys so close.

Dwight strolls across the hall outside the kitchen, points upwards. I shift to see a staircase curving up one wall, wide and ostentatious. The kind of thing a well-dressed lady might slowly descend to greet a party full of guests. Alvin steps up next to Dwight and whispers something, and they both giggle like schoolboys. I shake my head. I can't afford these distractions.

"Proceed with caution," Michael says from behind me, standing in the open back door, silhouetted by the sunshine outside.

I ignore him too.

My feet are silent on the tile floor as I stalk to the kitchen door, look past Dwight and Alvin. The hallway is dominated by the large staircase on one side, huge white double doors leading into a large reception room on the other. I can see fancy furniture inside, a ridiculous chandelier glittering. Edging around I see that it's empty. Light pours in through glass panels in the ostentatious front entrance dead ahead, dust motes dance and gleam.

"Up, fool," Sly says, sitting in a gold and satin chair by the front door. Marijuana smoke wreathes his head, jets from his nostrils in two thick streams.

I narrow my eyes at him, at Dwight and Alvin.

"You wondering why they're helping you?" Officer Graney asks from the bottom stair. "It's because they love the mayhem. The blood and the violence. And be honest, you love it too. It fuels you. Fulfills you. You thrive on it."

Fuck Graney and his philosophizing. I push by him and edge up the stairs, leaning back against the wall to point my gun at the landing above. I'm nearly at the top when something tickles in my hindbrain.

"Duck," Michael says casually.

I flinch to one side as rapid pistol fire breaches the silence. A tall vase beside me shatters into a million shards, chunks of plaster and wood spit out of the wall where I'd been standing a second before. I saw two muzzle flashes, some ten feet apart. I can't respond to both, so I pump shots at one as I dive up another five stairs. A bark of pain makes me smile and then the corner of a wall protects me from the firing angle of the other. For now. The first one is down, his feet toes up in the doorway of a bedroom.

I feel the smile still on my face, remember Graney's words, and it fades.

The other shooter is breathing hard, the kind of rasp that accompanies a lot of weight. Nervous fat men can never hide once they're out of breath. Maybe this guy ran upstairs when the shooting started. By the sound, I judge distance and angle. The muzzle flash was low, so he must be crouching. Assuming he hasn't moved, which makes him an idiot, I tuck my gun around the corner and fire three shots.

He screeches like a little girl, then his panting rapidly increases and he's muttering, "Oh god, oh god, oh god!"

I chance a look and he's clutching his chest, running bright with blood. He is a big guy, morbidly so, and his jowls wobble with his panic. He looks up, startles, tries to raise his weapon at me, but he's dead before his fat ass slaps into the floorboards.

Everything is still and quiet again. I listen hard, can only hear birdsong outside, the soft sough of the breeze. The house makes tiny creaks and moans of age and settlement, something downstairs pings quietly. A clock ticks, unnaturally loud, in the bedroom now blocked off by the fat man's corpse.

That's six of them. More like it. Could there be more? This pistol has four more shots, then I have three more fully loaded. And I'm not scratched yet. Doing pretty well. Maybe I didn't fuck up.

Crouching on the top step, protected from the large part of the house by the corner of the wall, I feel reluctant to move again. There are two doors in view in front of me, one with Toes Up lying half in and half out, the other closed. Could be a cupboard, a bathroom. Could be a room with a dozen armed men in it. And I have no idea what lies the other way.

Michael is sitting on the step below me, looking up. "Gonna chance it?"

"You could help me."

He smiles sadly, shakes his head. I take a deep breath, lay low to the floor of the upstairs landing, and quickly look around the corner. Gunfire booms, the wall and carpet kick and splinter as I whip back into cover. Something burns above my left eyebrow and hot blood is running in rivulets over my cheek, dripping onto my shoulder. Fuck, that was close. Someone up there is a good shot.

But I saw the layout. The landing extends along with two doors on either side and double glass doors at the end opening out onto a small veranda. I remember that from the outside, just a semicircle with a white railing fence, big enough for a small table and two chairs maybe. Somewhere for a quiet breakfast or afternoon tea.

Of the two doors nearest on either side, one is closed, the other filled with the obese corpse. The next two are both open and shooters sit in both, at least one on either side. The guy who nearly killed me is crouched on that tiny balcony, aiming through the glass doors. So three of them. At least. Still Charles and Vernon himself unaccounted for. But three others fanned out with complete coverage of my course, one of them an excellent shot. Presumably Vernon is in one or other of those open rooms, cowering but well-protected.

Maybe my luck just ran out.

Michael is gone, and Officer Graney is leaning against the closed door I can see from where I'm sitting. "You wanna know the odds?" he asks me.

I try to ignore him, but he goes on.

"Most gun battles, like this, it's momentum that keeps a shooter successful. Once they stop to think, to hunker down and regroup, that's usually when it's all over. They eventually try to move again and then they get shot. We train that way, to put ourselves in a position that makes the shooter stop and think, then we've got him. So. What are you thinking about?"

I shake my head, look away from him. Adrenaline surges in my system, blood thrums through my veins. My breathing is calm and measured, but my heart vibrates like a jackhammer. If I pop out again, that sharpshooter on the balcony will get me for sure. He's only about twenty feet away. As I shift on the stair, shattered ceramic grinds under my feet. Another of those tall vases stands a little further down the stairs, about three feet high, maybe a foot in diameter. As carefully as possible, not taking my eyes from the landing above, I shift step to step down to it and test its weight. Not too heavy at all.

Without stopping to think about it, I switch out to a fresh, fully-loaded pistol and carry the vase back up, my shoulder pressed to wall. I close my eyes, think about the distance, the angle, the width of the corridor up there. I'll only get one chance and I have to kill that fucker and hope the other two don't get a drop on me in the moments between.

The bullet wound across my forehead burns and my head is starting to pound, feels like my skull is swelling fit to crack. I breathe it down, mentally run through once more, then move.

My left hand launches the vase around the corner and it sails, spinning horizontally as I duck out behind it. Sharpshooter's eyes are wide as he both fires and raises his arm to block the incoming missile. It's enough, pulling his shot wide and I pump the trigger. My shots shatter the vase at the moment it collides with him. He staggers back, crying out as his arm and chest explode with blood. There's a crash as he backs into the small table, it tips, his legs flip up and he's gone, over the railing.

I'm already ducking back into cover before I hear his body hit the patio paving below, but it's masked anyway by gunfire from the doors either side. Two flares of pain makes me yelp, one in my left upper arm, one in my hip. I fire randomly left and right as I duck back behind the wall, then grit my teeth against the burning pain, gasping for breath, forcing down the adrenaline that narrows my vision and makes my hands shake.

The shot to my hip is a graze, hurts like fuck, but barely even bleeding. The arm is a different matter, the bullet punched right through the muscle of my triceps, my sleeve already soaked in blood. It hurts like hell to move that arm even slightly. I tear off my T-shirt from under my jacket, use the adrenaline and fury to wrap up the wound tight, stem the blood loss as best I can for now. Sharpshooter is down, but those other two are still there and I'm running out of time and blood. I wipe my head, my hand comes away red and dripping. At least it's to one side, not flooding my eye.

I tuck my injured left arm into my jacket to immobilize it. Thank fuck I'm right-handed. I take a deep breath. This has to end.

"He down?" a voice says from above.

"Did you get him?"

"Yeah, definitely. But I don't know if it was well enough to kill him. You?"

"Dunno."

Might be I can use this. I groan weakly, gather saliva in my mouth and cough wetly. I've heard enough dying men to know the sounds they make. Hopefully these goons have too.

There's a soft laugh. "That sounds promising."

"You go, I'll cover."

"*You* fucking go!"

"Jesus. All right."

Idiots. I cough and groan again, weaker this time, barely enough for them to hear. But just enough.

There's a shuffle of feet on the runner rug that covers the center of the hallway, a shadow appears on the wall opposite. I press myself hard against the wall at my back. As the shadow moves almost close enough to see, going slow as a nervous tortoise, I pop around the wall and empty three shots, gut, chest, head. His face is anger and shock, then I'm grabbing his falling corpse with my left hand, screaming at the pain in my arm, and holding him against me as a shield. He bucks and shifts as bullets from his pal riddle him, then I twist and empty my clip into the open door now I know which one it is. He dies with a furious, "*Fuck!*" and then everything is still and silent again.

Breathing hard, willing myself not to pass out from the pain, I tuck my injured left arm back into my jacket and stand there with a fresh gun held out before me. Slowly the blackness recedes a little from my eyes, my ragged breath the only sound. Even the birds outside have fallen silent, probably flown far away from the racket of explosions in the house.

So was that eight or nine? I've lost count, but it feels like enough. How many men could Vernon have gathered in the past week? How many would be here?

"Just you and me now, Vernon?" I say loudly. "And good old Charles, with his tongue up your ass."

There's a soft bark of laughter from the room on the left. "Fuck me, Eli. You're still alive? Again you decimate my associates in my own home."

Red attempts to replace the black in the edges of my vision and I gasp a deep breath before saying, "No number is enough to account for what you took from me." I move towards the open door. A study begins to reveal itself, shelves of leather-bound books, a red leather wing-backed chair, standard lamp. One end of a dark wood desk. I imagine Vernon is sitting or standing behind the desk, a weapon leveled at the doorway. Charles is probably tucked close to the wall near the door, at an oblique angle to ambush me as I enter.

"I was having a bad day," Vernon says.

"You fucking cunt."

"One thing you have proven beyond any doubt, Eli, is what an asset you'd be to anyone. I'd be a fool to keep you as an enemy. What is it you want?"

"I want you dead."

"Come now. There's better than killing. I'm on the back foot right now, I don't deny it. I have some…spot fires to put out from that idiot Tweezer blabbing. But I'm getting things organized. And I still have enormous wealth, Eli. I can give you virtually anything. Name your price."

"Walk to the doorway of this office, your empty hands held out in front."

"But why would I do that unless you can convince me you won't simply execute me?"

"Then we appear to be in a stand-off, as I'm sure you're armed."

His façade cracks. "Of course I'm armed, you pissant piece of shit!"

Movement catches my eye. The doors to the small balcony open inwards, panels of smooth glass. I can see him, reflected faintly, ghost-like, as the lowering sun lights his study. He is behind his desk, standing slightly to one side, a pistol leveled at the door. I shift ever so slightly left and right, wincing against pain and adrenaline, fighting the dizziness of blood loss. I can't see anyone else. It's a fifty-fifty guess which side of the door Charles will be on. Best guess is behind the door itself.

I relax, let my mind operate autonomous of thought, reversing angles, estimating distance. "Tell you what," I say. "How about…" Then I'm moving.

I duck around the doorframe and fire. Vernon yells as my shot takes the gun clean out of his hand, even as it goes off. Plaster falls from the ceiling as his shot goes wild, then he's cradling a bloody hand and snarling at me as I body-check the door back to slam Charles. But the door bounces off the wall, Charles nowhere else to be seen.

"Fuck you, Eli!" Vernon growls.

I'm an idiot.

I step away from the door, turning back to the hallway, but I'm too late. Light flares in my left eye, closely followed by a blast of pain and shock, as Charles flies across the hall from the room opposite and hits me. On instinct, as I spin away I pump my right elbow that way, feel it crack satisfyingly into a nose. Charles grunts and staggers back. What a fucking fool I am, hurting and hopped up on the action, but I should have known to check the other rooms as I went. I assumed Charles would stay close to Vernon. Assumptions get people killed. After all this, one ultimate fuck-up to end it all.

But Charles is a fool too. Following my elbow, my arm opens out, the pistol tracking to Charles's wide-eyed face. He expected his hit to knock me out. He should have shot me. Last mistake he'll make, I'm tougher than old boots when it comes to being KO'd. My vision is crossing, vertigo makes the walls tilt, but at point-blank range I blow his face into mincemeat then spin back to Vernon before Charles hits the floor.

But it's too late.

Vernon has another gun drawn and it booms. He's holding it left-handed, his right hand ruined and bleeding from my shot to his previous weapon, but even wrong-handed he's good enough to tag me. Pain flares again, this time in my right arm, near the shoulder. My gun drops from nerveless fingers.

Fuck it, so close! I slide down the wall, scrabbling for one of the guns in my boots despite the searing pain. I daren't look at the damage, but the agony makes my vision cross, my fingers aren't working properly, then Vernon is over the desk and aiming down at my head from only a yard away. Just beyond my reach.

His face is a mask of fury. "Even Charles? He was my best man."

I grunt, force a laugh. "Looks like I was your best man, fucker." Then I'm yelling at him. "*Maybe you shouldn't have murdered my family!*"

He smiles, shakes his head. "It didn't have to be this way, Eli. Are we not civilized beings?"

I'm incredulous, despite impending death. "No, we are clearly not. We're animals who wear clothes and pretend at some purpose, some perceived higher calling, when our brutality makes liars of us time and again." I have no idea where it's coming from, but the words pour out of me. "I mean, sure, some individuals can be virtuous, even civilized, but humanity, en masse, is no better than a well-dressed pack of hyenas, chattering excitedly around whatever carcass it's managed to subjugate this time. And that's the best of people, even those only concerned with themselves, ignoring so much suffering. And people like us? We are *far* from the best of humanity. We're among the worst, lying all the time to conceal our true natures even from ourselves."

Vernon tilts his head to one side. "So eloquent all of a sudden? And so cynical."

"But no less true."

"And all so pointless, now that you're going to die. A fucking mess you've made here, but I'll rise again, as I always do. You can't finish me, Eli. I'm untouchable. Immortal."

"You really believe that, don't you?"

He gestures loosely around. "See for yourself." He raises the weapon and lines it up to my face, taking his time to aim well left-handed.

As I brace for the final shot, I see the ghosts lined up along one side, all five of them, grinning.

"Ask him about the time he was raped in the can when he

was a teenager," Alvin says. "A skinny con, drunk on moonshine, called him sweet honey."

Alvin is older than the others, been around a while. As he says this I remember that he knew Vernon's father, the previous generation of this messed up family.

"Untouchable?" I ask Vernon. He raises an eyebrow at me. "Like that time you got fucked in the ass by a scrawny fucker who stank of jail-brewed moonshine and called you his sweet honey?"

Vernon's mouth drops open a fraction. "How can you know that?"

"I know Vernon tried to fuck my mom and she kicked him in the balls and ran away as he screamed like a little girl," Michael says with a laugh. They're enjoying Vernon's discomfort now, maybe given that my death is guaranteed.

"Or that time Mrs. Privedi made you think your nuts had burst when she kicked them?" I ask Vernon, hoping my embellishments ring true.

His brow creases. "How much did you fuckers all gossip? Is that how loose information is in my crew?"

"He came to my place once and raped an eleven-year-old girl," Dwight says, and even he seems disgusted by that. It surprises me, but maybe they were related. Would that be enough to cause Dwight distress?

Ignoring the roaring pain in both arms, my head, my leg, I creep my fingers towards my right foot, tucked up underneath me where I collapsed against the wall. My right foot, and the gun tucked in that boot. "What about the child you raped just outside Jacksonville?"

Vernon's face creases, and I can see even he regrets that one. His left hand shudders as trembling set in.

"Yeah, not even a teenager, so tight and crying out in pain, but you saw it through anyway, didn't you." My fingers inch nearer the gun, almost touching it now.

"No one knows about that!" he roars. "Tell me! Before I fucking kill you, tell me how you know that!"

"You'd be amazed what I know."

"That piece of shit Dwight is long dead, he can't have told you! Can he?"

I shrug my left shoulder to draw his eye, ignoring the flare of pain in that arm, and my fingers close over the gun in my boot.

"I can see you reaching for that weapon!" Vernon screams, and kicks my right arm, where his bullet hit me.

Pain howls from fingertips to neck, I choke out a sob of agony, my hand numb and throbbing. Vernon jams his gun barrel hard against my temple.

"Well, fuck you and whoever leaked this shit about me! It's all over, time for a new chapter. I'm glad I'll get to start again."

Fuck it all. I squeeze my eyes shut, my body as tense as racquet strings.

"Hey, Vern," Carly says.

My eyes pop open and there she is in the doorway, the .38 in her hand, the cable tie nowhere to be seen. Vernon stares agape.

"Eat shit and die, Vernon."

She fires and Vernon's eye bursts in a spray of scarlet. The back of his head opens out, bright white shards of skull and gobs of pink brain spatter back across the room. I dive to one side, anticipating his reflex shot. It's deafeningly loud and plaster showers over me in a white cloud, then I'm scrambling away.

I back up against the wing-backed chair, fighting off the blackness of pain. Carly stands in the doorway, staring down at

Vernon, the .38 hanging forgotten at her thigh in a trembling hand.

"Ah, fuck me!" Dwight says, disgust plain. "You're gonna survive this after all, you suck-ass piece of shit?"

I manage to raise a middle finger at him and he fades.

"So unsatisfying," Alvin says, and he fades too.

Sly makes a disappointed tutting sound, blows out a huge cloud of joint smoke and disappears into it.

"Vernon may be dead," Officer Graney says. "But we'll catch up to you eventually." He points at me, pins me with one long index finger. "You can count on that."

Then he's gone, and only Michael is left. He walks over, crouches beside me, puts one hand on my shoulder. He smiles thinly, gently kisses my forehead. Is that forgiveness? When I open my eyes again, he's gone.

"It's done," Carly whispers, still staring at Vernon.

It's only her and I now, and a house full of corpses. I can't speak. I swallow hard, wait. Eventually she turns her eyes to me.

"You were faking it," she says.

"What?"

"Fucking blanking out! You faked it. After everything, all we'd done, you still didn't think I was strong enough." There's a slight bruise on her chin from where I hit her.

"I just wanted to protect you from—"

"Fuck you! You would have died here and I'd be left to go back to him. Could you not tell I had the strength to be here? Surely I'd proven that."

I look at the floor, ashamed. She's right. "I'm glad you came."

"Fortunately, I kept a small knife in my sock ever since I first got a chance to shop, just in case you went weird and tied me up again. I cut the tie easily enough, took a while to stop feeling sick from being knocked the fuck out!" I wince. "Then I banged on the trunk for ages until the seat behind Kevin shifted and I realized I could get out there."

"In case I didn't come back." It sounds so lame now. "And Kevin?"

"I cut him free and told him to go home. He was going to walk to the highway and hitch back." She crouches and starts checking me over, dressing my wounds with Vernon's shirt, Charles's shirt, torn into strips. "Fucking hell, Eli."

"I got pretty close."

"It's a massacre out there, but you would have fucked up at the last minute. Fallen at the last hurdle."

I hiss between my teeth. "Story of my fucking life."

She keeps glancing back at Vernon as she fixes me up.

"You did it," I say after the fourth or fifth time. "He's not getting up again."

She looks at me with tears in her eyes. "You should have trusted me, and you did fuck up, but I would never have had that chance if it wasn't for you. You cleared the way here."

I smile weakly, unsure what to say.

Her tears breach, as much from the relief of finality as anything else, I imagine. "But now what will happen? A life on the run?"

I pick up the .38 from the floor beside her leg, put it in my jacket pocket. "You were never a willing accomplice. Tell them that. Keep telling them that."

"What?"

"When they find you here, you tell them I brought you along to get to Vernon, I killed everyone. It's almost entirely true. The whole time we were on the run, this past week, I've kept you tied up. Your bruises, those were from a couple of times you tried to escape, to come back to your husband."

"Eli…"

"And once I'd got him, I left you here and you don't know where I went. Which will be true."

"Eli, no. There must be something else."

"I've been a fuck-up my whole life. Even when I started making something good with my time, it was tied up inextricably with this fucker and this life. And it got them killed." I sniff, swallow hard. "Caitlyn and Scottie. They died because of me. I can't fix that." The pain of their loss roars louder than the bullet holes riddling me.

"So what will you do?"

"No idea. Something. Hide, drift, do what I can, where I can, try to atone for my myriad sins. And when they eventually catch me, I'll back up your story. You're safe from all this now. You're free. If nothing else, I've done that much."

I haul myself to my feet, blinking against the pain, the exhaustion, the dreggy comedown of fading adrenaline. Carly jumps up, grabs my arm but I shake her off.

"You're too hurt!"

"I'm tougher than you think. I know a guy in New Orleans, he'll fix me up, no questions asked. And he's not associated with Vernon. An independent guy."

She starts to speak again and I hold up my hand to stop her. "Don't follow me. Give it fifteen minutes, then call the police. Get them out here, tell them our story. You'll be free once all the bullshit gets worked through, you know you will."

"Eli, please."

"Seriously, don't follow. Okay?"

She stares at me hard for several moments, like she's trying to commit every line of me to her memory. Eventually she nods once. "Okay. Thank you." She leans up on tiptoes and kisses my cheek, comes away with blood-stained lips.

I huff a soft laugh. "You're welcome."

I don't look back as I stagger off through the house. It's a struggle to get back over the fence, but I manage, and the relief of falling into the driver's seat of the car is almost enough to finish me. Refusing to pass out, I start the engine and head towards New Orleans. I wasn't lying about the doctor there.

* * *

I'm sitting in bar in Ottawa, slowly drinking a cold beer, when I next hear Carly Sykes's name. It's been eighteen months since I left Vernon's house near Lake Maurepas. I'm used to the heavy ponytail of hair brushing my back, dyed jet black, and the thick beard that comes past my collar line now. Not yet used to the holes in my life where Caitlyn and Scottie used to be, but coping. I'd been ignoring the TV set burbling away in the corner until I heard, "Carly Sykes, infamous for being central in the botched kidnapping massacre in Louisiana a year and half ago, and heir to the Sykes fortune, was upbeat when she left court this afternoon."

I turn on my stool, and there she is: radiant, powerful. She looks stronger than ever, hair grown out again, back to her natural color. "It's a great relief to put all this behind me," she says, and my eyes narrow at the practiced voice, the familiar turn of phrase. "I'll be glad to get back to business as usual. Thank you. No further comment."

She breezes past the flashing cameras and microphones being thrust at her, a soft smile fixed in place, and ducks into a waiting limo.

The newscaster's voice drones over the top. "The so-called fresh power in organized crime in the American south, Carly Sykes maintained her innocence throughout proceedings. The case was thrown out for lack of evidence, fallen apart, some say, after the sudden car crash death of a key witness."

I tune it all out again. I've tried not to think about her for a year and a half, and I don't plan to start now. She's a pro, I'll give her that. I've seen Vernon do the same thing half a dozen times in the past. Looks like she's inherited Vernon's empire along with his fortune. I'd hoped for better, can't help wondering if she's the abuser now. Was it all for nothing? Maybe she's going to be as bad as Vernon ever was. Or perhaps she'll be a new breed, a benevolent dictator. I guess it doesn't really matter. It's all just people feeding off each other, no better than a well-dressed pack of hyenas.

END

ABOUT ALAN BAXTER

ALAN BAXTER IS A BRITISH-AUSTRALIAN AUTHOR who writes supernatural thrillers and urban horror, rides a motorcycle and loves his dogs. He also teaches Kung Fu. He lives among dairy paddocks on the beautiful south coast of New South Wales, Australia, with his wife, son, dogs and cat. He's the multi-award-winning author of several novels and over seventy short stories and novellas. So far. Read extracts from his novels, a novella and short stories at his website – www.warriorscribe.com – or find him on Twitter @AlanBaxter and Facebook, and feel free to tell him what you think. About anything.

MORE DARK FICTION FROM
GREY MATTER PRESS

———————————

"Grey Matter Press has managed to establish itself as one of the
premiere purveyors of horror fiction currently in existence."

- FANGORIA Magazine

———————————

CHICAGO

MISTER
WHITE

THE NOVEL

**DO
NOT
SPEAK
HIS
NAME**

JOHN C.
FOSTER

MISTER WHITE
BY JOHN C. FOSTER

In the shadowy world of international espionage and governmental black ops, when a group of American spies go bad and inadvertently unleash an ancient malevolent force that feeds on the fears of mankind, a young family finds themselves in the crosshairs of a frantic supernatural mystery of global proportions with only one man to turn to for their salvation.

Combine the intricate, plot-driven stylings of suspense masters Tom Clancy and Robert Ludlum, add a healthy dose of Clive Barker's dark and brooding occult horror themes, and you get a glimpse into the supernatural world of international espionage that the chilling new horror novel *Mister White* is about to reveal.

John C. Foster's *Mister White* is a terrifying genre-busting suspense shocker that, once and for all, answer the question you dare not ask: "Who is Mister White?"

"*Mister White* is a potent and hypnotic brew that blends horror, espionage and mystery. Foster has written the kind of book that keeps the genre fresh and alive and will make fans cheer. Books like this are the reason I love horror fiction." — Ray Garton, Grand Master of Horror and Bram Stoker Award®-nominated author of *Live Girls* and *Scissors*.

"*Mister White* is like Stephen King's *The Stand* meets Ian Fleming's James Bond with Graham Masterton's *The Manitou* thrown in for good measure. It's frenetically paced, spectacularly gory and eerie as hell. Highly recommended!" — John F.D. Taff Bram Stoker Award®-nominated author of *The End in All Beginnings*

GREY MATTER
P R E S S

greymatterpress.com

"Paul Kane is a first-rate storyteller."
— Clive Barker, Bestselling author of
The Hellbound Heart and *The Scarlet Gospels*

BEFORE

PAUL KANE

BEFORE
BY PAUL KANE

In 1970s Germany, a mental patient at the end of his life suddenly speaks for the first time in years. A year later in Vietnam, a mission to rescue a group of American POWs becomes a military disaster.

In present day England, the birthday of college lecturer Alex Webber sends his life spiralling out of control as a series of disturbing hallucinations lead him to the office of Dr. Ellen Hayward. And things will never be the same again for either of them. Hunted by an immortal being known only as The Infinity, their capture could mean the end of humanity itself…

Part horror story, part thrilling road adventure, part historical drama, Before is a novel like no other. Described as "the dark fantasy version of Cloud Atlas," Kane's Before is as wide in scope as it is in imagination as it tackles the greatest questions haunting mankind—Who are we? Why are we here? And where are we going?

The author and editor of more than sixty books, Kane's work includes *Sherlock Holmes and the Servants of Hell*, *Lunar*, *The Rainbow Man*, the Arrowhead trilogy (later released as the *Hooded Man* omnibus), *The Butterfly Man and Other Stories*, *Hellbound Hearts*, *The Mammoth Book of Body Horror*, *The Hellraiser Films and Their Legacy* and more. His work has been optioned and adapted for the big and small screen, including for US network television.

"Paul Kane is a first-rate storyteller, never failing to marry his insights into the world and its anguish with the pleasures of phrases eloquently turned."
— Clive Barker, author of *The Hellbound Heart* and *The Scarlet Gospels*

"I'm impressed by the range of Paul Kane's imagination. It seems there is no risk, no high-stakes gamble, he fears to take… Kane's foot never gets even close to the brake pedal." — Peter Straub, author of *Ghost Story*

GREY MATTER
P R E S S

greymatterpress.com

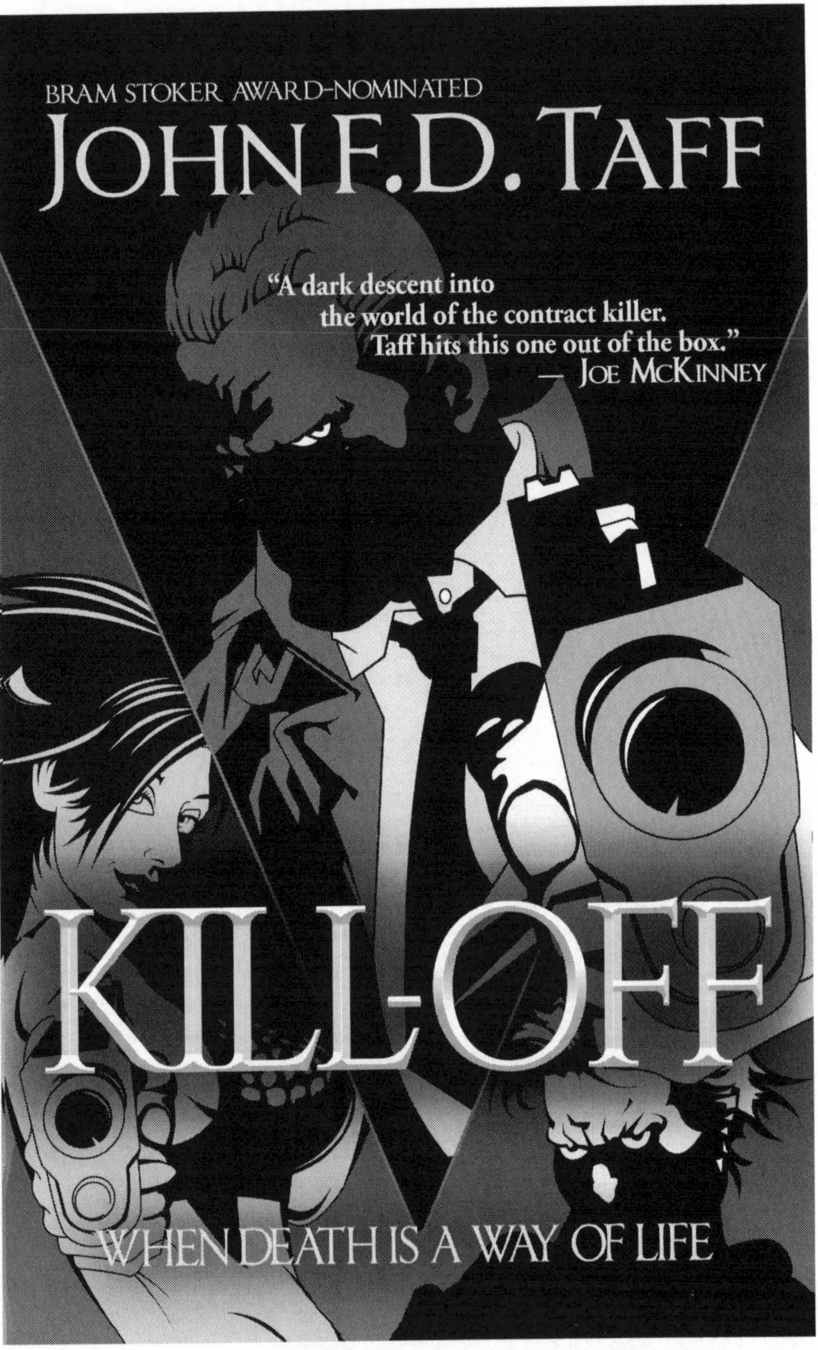
BRAM STOKER AWARD-NOMINATED
JOHN F.D. TAFF
"A dark descent into the world of the contract killer. Taff hits this one out of the box."
— JOE MCKINNEY
KILL-OFF
WHEN DEATH IS A WAY OF LIFE

KILL-OFF
BY JOHN F.D. TAFF

Would you kill someone — *anyone* — if you knew you could get away with it?

David Benning's life is unraveling. Unemployed, running low on cash and with the responsibility of caring for a father struggling with Alzheimer's, he finds himself blackmailed by a shadowy cabal with mysterious and deadly goals.

Known only as "The Group," David quickly learns they breed killers. Turning everyday people into accomplished assassins with unusual targets. As he's dragged farther down into this dangerous world of secrets, guns and payoffs, their true motives are slowly, chillingly revealed.

With nowhere to run, David can trust no one, not even the woman he's been sent to kill...and has grown to love. Can they work together to free each other from the deadly grip of this lethal game?

Kill-Off is a tough, no-nonsense and inescapable thriller in the vein of Richard Stark's *The Hunter* or James Cain's *The Postman Always Rings Twice*.

In *Kill-Off* death is a way of life.

GREY MATTER
P R E S S

greymatterpress.com

THE **REAL MONSTERS** ARE IN YOUR MIRROR

FROM BRAM STOKER AWARD® NOMINATED EDITORS

ANTHONY | SHARON
RIVERA | LAWSON

PEEL BACK THE SKIN

EDITED BY ANTHONY RIVERA & SHARON LAWSON

They are among us.

They live down the street. In the apartment next door. And even in our own homes.

They're the real monsters. And they stare back at us from our bathroom mirrors.

Peel Back the Skin is a powerhouse new anthology of terror that strips away the mask from the real monsters of our time – mankind.

Featuring all-new fiction from a star-studded cast of award-winning authors from the horror, dark fantasy, speculative, transgressive, extreme horror and thriller genres, *Peel Back the Skin* is the next game-changing release from Bram Stoker Award-nominated editors Anthony Rivera and Sharon Lawson.

FEATURING:

Jonathan Maberry

Ray Garton

Tim Lebbon

Ed Kurtz

William Meikle

Yvonne Navarro

Durand Sheng Welsh

James Lowder

Lucy Taylor

Joe McKinney

Erik Williams

Charles Austin Muir

John McCallum Swain

Nancy A. Collins

Graham Masterton

GREY MATTER
PRESS

greymatterpress.com

COMING SOON
FROM GREY MATTER PRESS

Devouring Dark — Alan Baxter

Little Black Spots — John F.D. Taff

The Madness of Crowds: The Ladies Bristol Book #2 — Rhoads Brazos

The Isle — John C. Foster

AVAILABLE NOW
FROM GREY MATTER PRESS

Before — Paul Kane

The Bell Witch — John F.D. Taff

The Devil's Trill: The Ladies Bristol Book #1 — Rhoads Brazos

Dark Visions I — eds. Anthony Rivera & Sharon Lawson

Dark Visions II — eds. Anthony Rivera & Sharon Lawson

Death's Realm — eds. Anthony Rivera & Sharon Lawson

Dread — eds. Anthony Rivera & Sharon Lawson

The End in All Beginnings — John F.D. Taff

Equilibrium Overturned — eds. Anthony Rivera & Sharon Lawson

I Can Taste the Blood — eds. John F.D. Taff & Anthony Rivera

Kill-Off — John F.D. Taff

Little Deaths: 5th Anniversary Edition — John F.D. Taff

Mister White: The Novel — John C. Foster

The Night Marchers and Other Strange Tales — Daniel Braum

Ominous Realities — eds. Anthony Rivera & Sharon Lawson

Peel Back the Skin — eds. Anthony Rivera & Sharon Lawson

Savage Beasts — eds. Anthony Rivera & Sharon Lawson

Secrets of the Weird — Chad Stroup

Seeing Double — Karen Runge

Splatterlands — eds. Anthony Rivera & Sharon Lawson

Suspended in Dusk II: Anthology of Horror — ed. Simon Dewar

MANIFEST RECALL

ALAN BAXTER

MANIFEST RECALL

ALAN BAXTER